George Morley Vickers

Ballads of the Occident

George Morley Vickers

Ballads of the Occident

ISBN/EAN: 9783744786683

Printed in Europe, USA, Canada, Australia, Japan

Cover: Foto ©Andreas Hilbeck / pixelio.de

More available books at **www.hansebooks.com**

BALLADS

OF

THE OCCIDENT

BY

GEORGE M. VICKERS

PHILADELPHIA, PA.
THE PARKVIEW PUBLISHING COMPANY
1898

TO HER GRACE

THE DUCHESS OF MARLBOROUGH

In testimony of the friendship
entertained for England by America,
which, although not generally appre-
ciated, lives ready to assert itself in
the time of need, I most respectfully
dedicate this volume.

GEORGE M. VICKERS

INTRODUCTION.

❧ ❧ ❧

THE poems contained in this collection do not include all that I have written, yet many of the pieces will be recognized by more than one aspirant for elocutionary honors, and enough lyrics are given to furnish an ample variety of themes. If upon the subject of patriotism I have been too prolific, my only apology is that I am an American.

THE AUTHOR.

CONTENTS.

8 *Contents.*

LYRIC POEMS.

BALLADS OF THE OCCIDENT.

Lost in the Mountains.

See you that yellow thread, that, snake-like, winds
High up the mountain side, now hid, now seen,
Now lost to view amid the shelving crags
And stunted pines? That is a rugged pass,
Called, hereabouts, The Devil's Trail. Just where
We stand, I stood one Autumn day, and heard
The legend from an aged mountaineer,
And, as my mem'ry serves me, word for word,
Like this the story ran:

                Mark Lysle, a rich,
Eccentric widower, and Maud, his child,
Long years agone, lived in that house whose red
Roof peeps from yonder clump of trees; and though
You see a light, blue plume of smoke above
The chimney top, yet other hearts now sit

About the hearth and watch its glow, for that
Bright fire which blazed when Lysle held sway,
    died out
One stormy night, never to burn again.
For miles and miles, which way you went, the
    fame
Of Lysle would greet your ear; his courtesies,
His open house and hospitalities,
Were themes discussed no less than were his
    quick
Resentment of a fancied slight, his fierce,
Hot temper, when aroused, or swiftness to
Avenge a wrong. But those who knew his child,
Who saw her pure, white brow, her gold brown
    hair,
And read the truth within her hazel eyes,
Deemed her in ev'ry trait of character
His antipode, his very opposite—
A lion him, and her a sweet gazelle.
Together lived they in that red-roofed house,
He, father, brother, lord and slave by turns:
She, ever steadfast, mild, obedient,
So like her mother—an exotic frail,
A Northern lily 'neath a Southern sun.

One Victor Dale, whose acres joined, and
    stretched
Far west from Lysle's estate; whose negro huts

Gleamed white amid the evergreens; the man
Her father called his chosen friend, this man,
Her senior by a score of years, and ill
Of feature, sought the maiden's hand, nay,
    claimed
It by a compact with her father made
Before her mother's death. But Maud, sweet
    Maud,
Who knew not how to hate, whom duty bound,
Whose only statute was her father's will,
Thus far had viewed her marriage in the light
Of something that she might escape, a thing
She might avoid, that would not come to pass;
As those condemned to death will hope when hope
Is dead, so hung she on the rosy thought,
And comfort took in hoping that it would
Not be; and though his would-be gallantries
Oft filled her with disgust, and oft provoked
A loathing in her breast, she hated not.

Once, on a summer day, with book in hand,
Maud sat beneath a tree. Upon the porch,
Reclining on a bamboo chair, her father dozed:
A sudden cry aroused them both in time
To see a horse, with empty saddle, dash
Across the road and leap the hedge. While yet
They stood amazed some field hands moving
    slow,

Came up the shaded walk bearing between
Their swarthy forms the helpless body of
A man.   With almost woman's tenderness
Mark Lysle made haste to have the wounded
    youth
Borne to his choicest room, and summoned
    quick
A surgeon, nor would rest until assured
His uninvited guest was doing well,
As well as one with broken limb could do.
Thus Henri Clair, an artist, far from home,
Was thrust by fate upon a stranger's care.

The leaves have lost their summer hue of green;
The purple grapes in clusters thick hang low;
The grain is garnered, and a late bee wings
Its way across the porch. Young Clair and Maud
Stand side by side; the setting sun shines full
Upon their faces: pale is his and sad,
And hers all tenderness and sympathy:
His time to go has come; this night will be
His last beneath her father's roof.   In two
Short months, by merest chance, their youthful
    hearts
Have learned to beat as one, yet hopelessly.
Behind a tree two other forms crouch low;
Her father, and her suitor, Victor Dale.
They glide away unseen.

That night when all
Were gathered round the hearth, Mark Lysle,
In tones that fell like death upon the ears
Of those who heard him speak, announced
It as his will, that on the coming day
His daughter Maud should wed his chosen friend;
"And, sir," said he to Clair, "as you must deem
It time to go, I shall not press you to
Remain, but bid you speed upon your way,"
And then, with haughty bow, strode out.

"Farewell,
Until we meet again—" "No, Maud, we must
Not say good-bye; to leave you now would be
To part forever," then young Clair's voice sank
Into a whisper; then, with one pure kiss
In haste imprinted on her brow, he left
The room, and then the house

The tall, old clock
That in the hallway stood, was striking nine
As Maud stole out into the night. Dark clouds
Were rising in the west. The lightning flashed
From out the distant sky; the thunder boomed
And rattled off in echoes 'mong the hills;
The black mass rising soon obscured the stars
O'erhead; then plashing rain-drops told the storm
Had burst. "To wed the hand and not the heart
Is sin, far greater than to disobey.

2

May God forgive me if I err: my heart
Must be my guide.'' Thus murmured Maud, as all
Alone she sped across the fields to reach
Yon rugged pass where Clair had gone to wait,
That when she came they both might mount his steed,
And so avoid pursuit, none dreaming they
Would choose that fearful path for flight.

The sun
Shone bright. The wet grass gleamed as though bedecked
With gems. The storm had gone; the night had gone,
And she had gone, the star of Mark Lysle's home,
Gone—to return no more.

The dark night through,
Young Henri Clair, high on a rocky cliff
Had watched and listened for his promised bride;
Had bended to the rock his ear, had called,
Loud as he dared, ''Maud! I am waiting, Maud!''
But never came reply.
Again, ''Here, Maud!''
Then sobbed and sighed the wind, all else was still.
At dawn of day, and fearing that she could

Not brave the storm, all wan and pale he rode
Swift down the steep descent to learn the worst.
He scarce had reached the narrow valley road
Ere Lysle and Dale each bade him halt or die.
Then shouting loud, they called the negroes,
    swore,
And charged him with the maiden's death or
    worse.
"She's lost! O God, she's lost! Come, follow
    me!"
Cried Clair; then, struck with cruel spur, his
    horse
In terror bore him up the winding path.
"I come!" shrieked out his rival, Dale; "I
    come!"
And off he dashed, his livid face drawn grim
With jealous rage. Then followed Lysle, and then
The throng of blacks, like hounds unleashed.

                             A cry!
Again a cry of mortal pain was heard!
The throng pressed up, and round a jutting point,
Till came in view a level breadth of rock
That shelved and overhung a sheer descent
Of awful depth. There, like a sculptor's work
On pedestal of stone, young Henri Clair
Sat rigid on his steed and pointed down
The deep abyss. In horror peered they all

Below, where lay the object of his gaze—
The white, the lifeless form of Maud.

                    The spell
Was broke by one wild laugh from Henri's lips.
With curb he drew his horse erect; he threw
His mantel o'er its head, struck deep his spurs,
And with the shout, "My bride!" leaped down
    to death.

And to this day the story still is told
Of trav'lers, who, belated on the pass,
Have heard, when softly sobbed the wind, a voice
Call tenderly and low, "I'm waiting, Maud!—
Here, Maud!—Is that you, Maud?"

The Pilot's Bride.

"Deep locked in the ocean the secret lies
Of many a ship that ne'er will rise,
Yet 'tis easier far the world's wrecks to find
Than to guess one thought in a woman's mind."
Thus spoke Clyde Howe as he paced the deck
Of the pilot schooner Nancy.   "Neck
And neck I've been racing for Molly's love,
With the owner's son on the cliff above;
Sometimes she gives him a glance, a smile,
Then I get the same—if I wait a while;
The fact is I'm tired, and want to know
Which one of us two's to be Molly's beau."

Up on a headland bold and high,
Clean cut and backed by the deep blue sky,
Rested the mansion of Humphrey Lee,
Massive and grim as a fort could be;
And many's the skipper who sailing by
Has looked through his glass and wondered why
No flag, no sentry, nor gun was seen,
But only its magazine round and green,
Which,   though   to   the   sailors   bomb-proof
        appeared,
Proved only a moss-topped spring when neared.
Thus many from habit, and some in sport,
Oft spoke of the place as Humphrey's Fort.

On the gray stone flags of his portico
Old Humphrey Lee walked to and fro;
At times he would pause and look off to sea
Then turn and gaze at a shrub or tree,
Or cross to the wall at the headland brink,
Lean over the chasm and seem to think.
Far down the red rocks of the sheer abyss,
Where ever the wild waves seethe and hiss,
Old Humphrey long peered; then turned away,
When right in his path stood, laughing gay,
His son, young Vivian, tall and fair;
Handsome of form, and of haughty air.

The young man laughed till his cheeks were
        red,
He held his sides and then gasping said:
"Why, father, I've just been watching the race
'Twixt the frowns and smiles on your changing
        face;
And, asking your pardon, I'm forced to say
That by odds the dark frowns have won the day!"
"Aye, frowns, and too many, and smiles too few,
Where all might be smiles, were it not for you."
Then old Humphrey continued, more sad than
        stern,
"Vivian, my son, try some good to learn;
Be manly, and tell me both frank and true,
What is Molly, the fisherman's child, to you?"

"Well, really, I've thought not the matter o'er,
Since Molly's but one of a score or more
Of the people I speak to or friendly greet
When we pass in the roads or village street."
Then old Humphrey took Vivian's proffered
    arm,
And remarked that his question implied no harm,
"But," said he, "this morning I came to know
That the young woman's coming quite soon to
    sew;
She will stay for a week to help make and mend,
Though Aunt Leah will treat her as guest and
    friend."
"I see," laughed his son. And the sunset bright
Flooded Humphrey's grim fort in a golden light.

'Tis night, and the yellow May moon looks down
On the restless sea and the little town;
It shows on its face, in silhouette,
Two forms by the headland wall; and yet
An observer might easily reckon three,
Though the bended form's but a withered tree.
'Tis a lovely scene, and the ocean's roar
Blends sweet with the tale that's told once more.
"Molly," plead Vivian, "you soon must go;
I love you, then answer me yes—or no."
"I cannot. I love not," said Molly, "but when
The harvest moon shines, I will tell you then."

The trim schooner Nancy at anchor lay,
Her white sails furled and her crew away,
Away with mothers, with sisters and wives,
For pilots and sailors lead risky lives;
And though long or short, when the cruise is
    o'er,
Jack drops his anchor and skips ashore.
To the dim lit porch of a fisher's home
Slowly two earnest talkers come;
They sit on the worn bench side by side
Where the woodbines partly their faces hide.
"Clyde," 'tis Molly's low voice, "I will answer
    soon;
I will tell you one night by the harvest moon."

In the little port 'tis a holiday,
For the old to rest and the young to play.
The sun has gone down in a bank of red,
And a star or two peeps overhead;
Yet still at old Humphrey's Fort are seen
The villagers dancing upon the green.
On a strip of beach, mid the jutting rocks
Whose slippery sides stay the waves' fierce
    shocks,
A group of maidens are seeking shells,
By the rest unseen till their shrieks and yells
From the depths of the roaring gulf below
Bespeak their presence and fearful woe.

One moment's confusion, one answering cry,
Then all to the wall in their anguish fly;
First over its crest young Vivian springs,
Then follows Clyde Howe, as a loud cheer rings
From the men behind, who are slipping fast
Down the long rope ladder; and ere the last
Has touched the slant beach of crumbling shale
Horror strikes them all, and each cheek turns
    pale.
See! Clyde Howe in the angry billows leaps,
Is struggling hard with the tide that sweeps,
Sweeps Molly far out on a mountain wave,—
Sweeps both to their death, and a cold, deep
    grave!

"This purse of gold, and ten purses more,
To whoever brings safe that girl ashore!"
Young Vivian's voice has grown shrill with
    fear,
But no one remains his words to hear,
Save the women above, for the men have sped
For a lifeboat housed in the coast-guard shed.
Onward, yet onward, brave Clyde swims out,
Now lost in the trough, now tossed about;
And weaker, yet weaker the drifting maid
Still struggles, scarce seen in the twilight shade—
Now Clyde—now both in the gathering gloom
Drift swift from sight to their awful doom!

Hark! out from the shadows there comes a cry,
'Tis a shout of joy and of victory!
Old men and women gaze eager down
Where Vivian waits with an anxious frown
Huzza! 'tis the lifeboat, one stroke more,
And she rides the huge breakers safe to shore.
"Take this purse, brave Clyde," young Vivian
    said;
But the hero proudly shook his head,
And trembling they stood, nigh about to swoon,
When up from the sea came the harvest moon.
"Sweet Molly, will you be my prize" said
    Clyde;
And she answered, "Yes, I'm the pilot's bride."

Roderick Lee.

This is a wild, lone valley, and the road that
    threads it through
Is the loneliest road I know of, and I've traveled
    not a few;
Those hills on the left so barren, and yon tower-
    ing, rocky ridge,
Look down on a sluggish river that is spanned
    by a moss-grown bridge—
And nigh to the bridge like a sentry, a tall, gray
    chimney stands,
'Mid the wreck that time has buried 'neath the
    tangled weeds and sands.

In this valley three ruins moulder that were once
    three happy homes,
And where once fond voices mingled, now the sly
    fox fearless roams;
Then these locks were thick and glossy, that are
    now so sparse and gray;
Then I'd calmber these rocks as willing by night
    as I would by day—
But, if a royal sceptre, if the world were promised
    mine
To cross again this valley, I would shudder and
    decline.

(27)

Roderick Lee was a miller, and as grist was hard
    to find
Down in his old New Hampshire, he had little
    or naught to grind;
So, with his young wife blooming and his brown-
    eyed daughter Nell,
Together with two young farmers, he came to
    this place to dwell:
And many's the mile of prairie, and many's the
    forest drear,
That lay 'twixt the far-off Merrimack and the
    stream that ripples here.

Yet with a heart as buoyant and as brave as it
    was true,
Young Lee, 'mid the cheers at parting, bade his
    native town adieu;
Then came the weeks of toiling, aye, months,
    ere the scorching plain
Was crossed, and his eyes were greeted by the
    distant mountain chain;
But the white-topped, dusty wagons at last made
    their final stand,
And he knelt to breathe thanksgiving with his
    little pilgrim band.

Stay! even now in fancy, I can see their forms
    once more,
I can see their peaceful faces and the look of hope
    they wore—

Poor Kate and Nell and Edith, young Harry,
    Mag and Joe—
'Neath that oak I see them kneeling, tho' 'tis
    thirty years ago!
And long ere the hazy autumn had mellowed
    another year,
Our huts were built in the clearing, and our corn
    hung ripe in the ear.

Joe was a model husband, as fair Edith, his wife,
    well knew,
And Mag and her raw-boned Harry, lived as
    loving couples do;
But, as their homes were childless, very natural-
    like it fell
That these kind and worthy people thought the
    world of little Nell.
Many a time they kept her whole days 'gainst
    her mother's will,
First in the hut by the river, then in the hut by
    the hill.

Once in the chill November, when the slender
    moon hung low,
And the barren hill-tops yonder were clad in a
    gauze of snow;
Kate with a gleam of mischief in her bright and
    twinkling eye,
Started across the river to the hut of Joe, hard by;

And Roderick sat by the window, watching her
    out of sight,
Dreamingly watching the shadows of that chill
    November night.

Ere it had seemed a moment she again stood by
    his chair;
She had called at their neighbor's cabin, but
    Nellie had not been there.
Roderick slowly rising took his rifle from the
    rack,
For the road was wild and lonely and led through
    a forest tract;
Over the ruts and boulders, chatting, they strode
    along
Till the voice of raw-boned Harry was heard in
    a merry song.

"Singing for Nell's amusement," said the wife,
    as she hurried on;
"Pity," she added, musing, "that they have no
    child of their own."
Soon with a hearty greeting they were met at
    the cabin door,
"And where is your little daughter?" asked
    Mag, as she scanned them o'er.
"Question your good man, Harry, for I'll ven-
    ture that he can tell,"
Said Kate, then smiling added, "we must stop
    lending little Nell."

Mag, with a playful gesture drew the bedroom
    screen aside,
"See!" she exclaimed, "she's not here; now I
    hope you are satisfied."
"Come, Maggie, come, don't trifle, for the hour
    is growing late;
I know that the child is hiding; would you have
    us longer wait?"
Thus queried Kate, half pleading, when a look
    akin to fear
Stole over the face of Harry as he said, "She is
    not here!"

"Not here! O God protect her!" with a gasp
    young Roderick cried,
And his pale wife like a statue, mute with fright,
    stood at his side.
'Twas but a single moment, yet it seemed like an
    age to wait
Ere Mag and Kate with their husbands filed out
    through the open gate;
Dark was the night as a dungeon, for the moon
    had sunk away,
And the far-off cries of a panther filled each
    breast with dread dismay.

On through the gloomy forest like a band of
    ghosts they sped,
Silently, save when the mother sobbed, or a twig
    snapped 'neath their tread;

"Hark!" whispered tall, gaunt Harry, and they
    stood with heads bent low,
While faint on the air of midnight came shrieks
    of pain and woe.
"Hello! hello!" cried Harry; but they heard no
    voice reply—
"Heavens! what means that crimson, that glow
    on the fleecy sky?

"See how it spreads and deepens! Look! our
    cabins are ablaze!"
Then Roderick paused in terror at the sight that
    met his gaze.
Light grew the wood about them; their shadows
    fell before,
For behind them on the hillside leaped the flames
    from Harry's door:
"On for your lives!" screamed Harry, "on for
    little Nell!"
Then, like an answering challenge, rose the dis-
    tant Indians' yell.

Bang! bang! "That's Joe replying; he'll fight
    'em game and well,"
Were the words that Harry uttered; "God spare
    my darling Nell!"
This from the pallid mother; and the settlers
    fairly flew
O'er the matted brush and boulders till the clear-
    ing came in view.

Oh, such a sight of ruin! oh, such a ghastly
    scene!
Stark, dead, lay Joe and Edith on the charred
    and trampled green.

Crouching down 'mid the bushes they watched
    the painted fiends,
Watched with the strange, grim calmness that
    despair so often lends;
"My child! my child!" then springing from
    the group like a startled deer,
Kate rushed o'er the red-lit clearing ere one
    could interfere—
The hideous, screeching cut-throats had captured
    little Nell;
But, when they saw her mother, they stood
    bound, as by a spell.

"Spare! oh, spare my darling! Here, pierce
    me, strike me dead!
Give back my child, my Nellie!" the frantic
    woman said;
Then on her panting bosom her daughter's head
    she laid,
Then both sank down in silence, looked up and
    mutely prayed;   [hell
That was the fatal signal, for on, like a sweeping
They came with knife and hatchet, with rifle-
    shot and yell.

3

Bravely they fought, yet vainly, that fated settler
    band,
Clubbing their empty rifles, meeting them hand
    to hand;
Roderick reeled and staggered, then fell 'neath a
    crushing blow,
And a whoop of fiendish malice told the triumph
    of the foe;
Then like a flash they vanished, and Roderick
    bleeding lay,
Hearing their yells grow fainter, till at last they
    died away.

Gray dawned the wintry morning on that awful
    scene of death,
And five cold brows of marble were kissed by its
    chilling breath—
God in His wisdom took them—save Nellie, who
    ne'er was found;
And all of them sleep in this valley, each 'neath
    a grassy mound.
Poor little Nell may be living, but if living she's
    dead to me;
Yes, the tale is indeed a true one—and my name?
    —is Roderick Lee.

Buzzard's Point.

Huge, fleecy clouds, like stately ships, drift by,
And in their wake come more to join the fleet
Now seeming anchored in the southern sky;
A hundred glassy pools reflect the sun,
For, save yon brook-like thread, the river bed
Is dry, and only sand and shale mark out
Where deep Ohio thunders to the sea.
Upon the rocky summit of a bluff
That juts far out from shore, two lovers sit
Beneath the shade of mingling beech and elm.
The man is young; the maid, almost a child;
Yet in the eyes of both is seen the fire
Of holy love, true love, that only dies
With life—
      Blue eyes and brown; hers blue, his brown.
And oh, how gloriously free their hair
Coquettes, streams off, now flutters back to kiss
Again; his chestnut dark to twine in sport
Amid her living gold.   Blow on, fair breeze;
Sing sweet, chirp low, ye merry birds, for here
Two hearts make solitude of all the world
That lies beyond their rosy world of love.
A tree trunk forms the seat whereon they sit,

And vines and shrubs a perfect bower make
The place, so wild and yet so beautiful:
Below them, full a mile, a log hut stands;
The forest trees, like giant infantry
Updrawn have formed a three-flanked hollow
    square
About the strip of clearing; further on
The river sweeps around a graceful bend
And hides its course amid the dense green leaves.
The lovers rise.   He places on her head
The rough straw hat that so becomes her fair
Sweet face, and then takes up his own broad felt
From off the ground.   They stand and look afar
Among the drifting clouds.   The birds chirp low;
Their plumage gay gleams bright, as flashing
    through
A patch of sunlight, swift they dart in glee.
How tame, how fearless in their native home.
See there, among the vines that twine that tree,
There, where his rifle rests!   What kind of bird
Is that?   Its plumes are gray; how slow it moves!
It glides away.   Perhaps it may come back.
Strange bird.   There, where his rifle rests—but
    see!
His rifle is not there, 'tis gone!
                         Whiz! Click!
And, as the tomahawk still trembles in
The tree, the startled lovers each spring back,

Then turn to see the scowling copper fiend
That clasps Ben Dowling's rifle in his hand.
No shriek escapes her firm-pressed lips, as calm,
Though deathly pale, the girl steps back a pace;
No sign of fear betrays her frozen heart:
She sees her lover slowly draw his knife,
Beholds the crouching savage raise the piece
To take delib'rate aim.   A dash, a flash
Of fluttering white, and she has leaped and grasped
The rifle in her small brown hands.

                            With yell
Of rage the red man springs aside to shun
The lover's keen-edged blade, then whipping
    out
His own long knife, with horrid grin prepares
To meet his foe.   The cunning dog keeps well
The lover in a line between himself
And that bright barrel resting on a branch;
For Mabel Earle is no mean shot, and with
Her finger on the trigger mutely bids
The painted wretch beware!   A moment's pause,
And now the work begins.   Thrust, guard,
    lunge, cut,
Now parry, clink! the sparks fly as their cold
Blades clash.   The Indian advances quick,
A sudden stroke. ''Lost! O my God, he's killed!''
Ben Dowling reels, the red stream trickles down
His face.   ''Kneel! Kneel! for life, stoop low!''

The girl
Is ashen white.   Clink! clink! more sparks.
   "O Ben,
My own, he's growing faint, he staggers—Oh!"
The savage strikes again.   The lover falls.
A shot—"There, murderer!"   The blue smoke
      veils
Her wet blue eyes—the red chief drops his knife,
He rallies, clutches at the air, spins round
And round, now nears the brink, is nearer still,
Still nearer, gone!
                  "Oh, speak to me," she cries,
As bending o'er her lover's form she wipes
The blood stains from his pallid face.   "Oh,
      speak
To me, but tell me that you live!   Ah, see!
He moves his lips!   Thank Heaven he lives!   His
      eyes
Unclose, he faintly smiles!   Ha, hark!"   "Ye
      ho!
Ye ho!"   "Saved, saved!" and placing both her
      brown
Hands to her lips she answers back the cry,
"Ye ho! ye ho!" and swoons away.
                              They come,
Her father and a trapper friend.   The thing
That first they see looks like a wounded bird,
A buzzard, hanging on a twig above

Them high; another glance and well they know
'Tis but the head-gear of an Indian,
Caught off as down he fell.

                  And thenceforth on,
Long after Ben and Mabel happy lived
And died, the place was known as Buzzard's
    Point.

The Trysting Well.

I.

"Why, Nellie, how's this?" said Farmer Brown,
Driving his team from the market town.
But never a word from her red lips fell,
As smiling she stood at the trysting well.
"Women is odd," the old farmer said,
And he cracked his whip and shook his head.
The farmer no sooner had left the place
Than a change came over the maiden's face;
The smile had gone like a rippling wave,
And the look on her face was sad and grave.
Then, shading her eyes with her small, white
    hand,
The dusty road and the fields she scanned;
She saw the late birds as they nestward flew,
And glanced at the shadows that longer grew;
She heard the faint strokes of the village bell,
Yet lonely she watched at the trysting well.

II.

Now old Farmer Brown loved to drink and smoke,
But the pride of his heart was to play a joke,
And scarce from the well had he passed away
When he met a young horseman hard riding and
    gay:

"Ah, lad," cried the farmer, "you're late, you're
    late,
Your lass I saw pass through the meadow gate!"
"True, Farmer Brown, I have been delayed
By a shoe cast off from this sorrel jade;
Though just what you mean by that last remark
Concerning a lass, why, I'm quite in the dark."
The young man colored and grasped his rein,
But to Farmer Brown his deceit was plain,
Aye, far beyond doubt, when he saw him strike
His mare till she flew down the dusty pike.
And the farmer winked as he saw him pass,
Like the wind, o'er the dewy meadow grass;
Yes, the sly old dog watched the horseman
    fleet
Till his form was lost in the village street.
Then loud on the air his wild laughter broke
At the big success of his clever joke.

III.

By the merest chance, on that eve it fell,
That a man strode up to the trysting well;
He had stopped at the moss-grown, limpid pool
To slake his thirst with its waters cool.
"Gerald!" He started, and made reply,
As a shadowy phantom caught his eye.
"Not Gerald, Miss Nellie," he quickly said,
"But I hope, for this once, I'll do instead."

Like a surging sea of crimson flame
The hot blood swift to her temples came.
Her lover's rival before her stood,
And she alone, in the dark'ning wood.
Below them the village lamp lights lay,
Cheering the gloom of the fading day.
"As I, too, am going the self-same way,
Allow me to be your escort, pray."
His voice was sincere, and implied respect,
And he drew his sinewy form erect.
Though her thoughts and fears were but half
    concealed,
There was nothing left but to bow and yield.

IV.

When the rider dashed off from old Farmer
    Brown
And rode through the streets of the little town;
When he hitched his mare to the garden tree
And looked for the face that he did not see;
When he heard that his Nellie was still away,
Then jealousy, love and wild dismay
For a moment held him a captive chained,
But the next, and his reason was full regained.
The round harvest moon o'er the hilltop lay
As on foot through the village he took his way.
He had gone not far when he met a sight,
That made him doubt that he saw aright.

No pistols were drawn, no duel was fought,
But a lesson was learned and a trick was taught;
And the three stood there in the moonlit town
Planning a penance for Farmer Brown.

V.

And it happened the very next market day
As he drove along on his homeward way.
Half the village turned out the old fellow to see
Tied wrong side up, to a hickory tree:
And they laughed and they shouted to hear him
     yell,
As he dangled right over the trysting well.

VI.

Farmer Brown still enjoys his sociable smokes,
But should you ever meet him—don't mention
     jokes.

Tom's Thanksgiving.

The smoke rose straight from the chimney
  Till lost in the autumn air,
And the trees round the little cottage
  Stood motionless and bare;
But within there was life and bustle,
  There was warmth in the kitchen stove,
And the smile of a patient woman,
  And the glow of a deathless love.

The cakes and pies on the dresser
  Stood ranged in a tempting row,
And the table-cloth on a chair-back
  Was smooth and as white as snow;
On the table, 'mid bags and baskets,
  A big, fat turkey lay,
For Tom, our Tom, was coming
  To spend Thanksgiving Day.

Yes, Tom had sent us a letter,
  The first that had come for years,
And we read it all over and over
  Till its lines were dimmed with tears:
The boy who had nigh disgraced us,
  Whose mem'ry was dead to some,
The wayward, the lost, was coming;
  Thank God, he was coming home.

To-day, as I think it over,
   The old scene comes back again,
And I see their anxious faces
   As plain as I saw them then;
I can see poor grief-bowed father
   Standing by mother's side,
Both peering out through the window,
   Trying their fears to hide.

I can see a manly horseman
   Dismount at the cottage door,
And remember the kindly message
   That from absent Tom he bore;
I remember how mother detected
   The cheat, and then swooned away;
And forever I'll still remember
   That sweet Thanksgiving Day.

The Cobbler of Lynn.

The lights burn dim.   A sea fog drifts in dank
And chill; the tavern doors are closed; and, save
The blinking, drowsy watchman on his rounds,
The town of Lynn lies fast asleep.

                       Loud, deep,
Barks out a near-by mastiff.   Shrill and faint
He's answered far away; now echoes come
From curs all o'er the town; the din grows less;
Now all is still.   The lights are blurred and dim;
The sea fog still drifts in, and still the town
Of Lynn lies fast asleep.

                One, two, clangs from
The belfry overhead with lazy stroke
And creak.   The clapper jangling with the bell's
Vibration seems the hour's dying gasp.
The watchman yawns and trudges down the
     street;
And still the town lies fast asleep.

                   An old
And toppling house, whose low, slant roof upholds
A field of moss, squats on a thoroughfare.
A rusty sign swings from the door, on which,
By day, is seen a yellow boot; beneath,
Upon the low stone step, wrapped in a shawl,

(46)

An infant slumbers sweet; within the house
An honest cobbler snores; and on you dark
And sobbing tide a dead young mother floats,
The cold waves kissing oft the marble brow
That human lips refused to press.

                   The years
That lie between that night and this bright morn
Are full a score. The sweetest face in Lynn
Is Marion's; the grandest eyes are hers;
A queenly form and grace: and yet she dwells
Not in a mansion, neither has she maids.
The cobbler more than once with joy and pride
Has thanked Saint Crispin for his generous gift
Of twenty years ago.—And who would not?
Beside his bench she stands this summer morn
And gayly chats; repeats the latest talk,
And fondly smooths his silver locks, while he,
With dark and horny hand takes up his awl
And plies his waxen thread.

                  Though every day
Was once to-day, and every day will be
To-day, yet only this is our to-day; its peace,
Its opportunities, its dearest hopes
May with it go, to come no more.

                  The blush
Has faded from New England's sky, and old
Nahant lies dark against the afterglow.

The cobbler's bench is vacant; on the wall
His apron hangs; for he has gone to meet
A stranger from Manhattan, at the inn.
But Marion is home. Step soft this way.
A spacious room with floor of well-worn oak;
An open door and window looking south;
A wide tile hearth; a simmering pot of tea;
A table snowy white, all set for three.
Within this room, that serves for banquet hall,
For parlor, kitchen, each in this and this
For each, with anxious face sits Marion.

'Tis late. The meal is still untouched, and tears
Are slowly trickling down the maiden's face.
Before the hearth, their shadows thrown across
The room, stand two determined men,—the old
And faithful cobbler, and a stranger tall,
Of proud, commanding mien. ''Well, then,''
    said he,
''If this young lady deems your ancient shop
And stinted means of greater value than
Her father's vast estate and revenue,
My duty is fulfilled.'' The cobbler speaks
No word, but looks upon the floor. ''Or if
She feels indebted for your generous care
And loathes to leave you all alone, her purse
Can recompense you well, quite well, and place
You far above the need of toil. I wait

Your answer.'' Keen the stranger's dark eyes
    search
The cobbler's troubled face. ''Ask Marion;''
The old man's voice is tremulous and low;
''Her welfare is the only recompense
I ask.'' Now in a firmer tone, ''But this
I say, she shall not go, nor stay, against
Her will.'' The stranger starts. ''How say
    you, miss?''
The maiden rises to her feet; her face
Is pale, her hazel eyes are wet. ''O sir,''
Her voice is sweet and clear, ''there are some
    debts
Which money cannot pay; and such a debt
I owe that aged man. You say you know
I am the one you seek, can prove it by
This locket and the name it bears; I grant
You that. Your story of my mother's life,
Her illness, her insanity, her flight
And unknown fate, until you learned it here;
My father's grief, his search of years, his last
Request, his death, may all be true; and though
Within my heart a something whispers that
It is but partly true, I also grant
You that; and once again refuse to leave
One who has more than father been to me;
And could my spirit mother speak, I know
She'd bless her child for being true. While life

4

Is mine, dear guardian, these hands are yours.''
The cobbler clasps her in his arms.   ''God bless
You, Marion,'' he sobs.   The stranger bows;
His dark eyes gleam, and with the single word,
''Enough!'' he passes from their sight.

                              The fierce,
Wild tempest passing o'er may rend the waves
To foamy shreds, but having past, leave not
A trace upon the tranquil sea; so clouds
Of grim adversity are followed oft
By sunny days of prosperous bliss.   Once more
Within the cobbler's home the calm
Routine of peaceful life holds sway.   The old
Affection, though, seems stronger grown; for she,
Sweet Marion, still closer clings to him,
Her aged guardian, and in the shop
Oft sits and sews, or talks the time away
Till candle-light.

                    But with the autumn comes
A change.   The maid has lost her sprightly air;
She mopes about, or stands and gazes far
Beyond her vision's range; again, she starts
And calls to forms unseen; she seldom smiles.
The cobbler sometimes leaves his bench with
        stealth
And watches her, as silently she plucks
The dead sprays from her marigolds, or wreathes

A garland bright of dahlias, in their strip
Of garden.   Now, in weird soliloquy
He hears her speak: "O mother, were you mad?
Am I insane?   What! money buy my love?
I cannot help but think the stranger was
My own—No, no!—Ah, Guardy! there you are!
I see you peeping there!"   And so the days
Now come and go within their home.

                          'Tis morn.
The town of Lynn is all astir.   The pale
And horror-stricken people stand in groups.
The history of twenty years ago
Repeats itself.   The dripping form, still fair
In death, of Marion is borne along
The street.   Found drowned; and that is all they
    know.

The cobbler could not live in gloom; his bright,
Warm sunshine gone, he drooped away and died.

Sigh not, weep not for Marion.   What you
Have heard was acted years and years ago,
And all the actors long have slept.   Weep not
For Marion, but rather give your tears
And charity to those who live and lack
A mother's love; the erring desolate,
Who perish for a kindly word.

Dead Man's Gulch.

It happened 'way back in the fifties
   When the country was crazy on gold,
When the gulches and hills near 'Frisco
   Were yielding their wealth untold;
It happened when men and women,
   Of every manner and kind,
Came seeking the yellow nuggets
   That the thrifty diggers mined.

The camp was of rambling shanties,
   With a single narrow street,
And a tall tree shaded the tavern
   And the crowd from the noon-day heat;
In a circle the miners were seated,
   A jury of fifty or more,
And the prisoner sat in a wagon
   In front of the bar-room door.

She was one of those wretched creatures
   Whose lives are made up of sin,
Whose crimes are all seen on the surface,
   But none of the good within.
Tom Scott was the judge and spokesman,
   And he briefly lined out his case
That the woman was guilty of murder,
   Cowardly, cruel and base:

A man had been found in a thicket
  With a bullet-hole through his head;
Still the blood from the wound was flowing
  But the spark of his life had fled:
While the party that found him wondered
  Who fired the fatal shot,
This woman was silently stealing
  Away from the dreadful spot.

No doubt she'd have robbed the body,
  But, hearing them, took alarm;
In her hand she still held this pistol,
  It was empty, the barrel was warm.
When the witnesses asked why she did it,
  She uttered a piercing shriek,
But in spite of their threats and questions
  Not a word would the woman speak.

An old man, pale and grizzled,
  Then pushed to the open place
In the circle of angry miners,
  And glanced at each threatening face.
"Let me speak, for I am a witness,
  And my strength is failing fast,
Let me speak for the sake of justice
  Ere the power to speak is past.

"Stop! Let us look behind us,
   Through the mist of time and tears,
Till we view the golden sunlight
   That in by-gone days appears:
Far away in the past, a maiden,
   The pride of her happy home,
Sings only of love's devotion,
   Dreams only of joys to come.

"Her heart has been won by a stranger,
   Who calls her his love, his life,
And vows that he wooes with honor,
   That he'll make her his darling wife;
But the old folks' hearts are heavy,
   For they see that he seems not true;
In spite of his words soft spoken,
   They fear that their child will rue.

"One morning they found a letter,
   On the open Bible it lay;
It asked for their kind forgiveness
   And told that she'd gone away.
The mother was broken-hearted,
   And the grief of them both was wild;
But the father kneeled down by the Bible,
   And swore that he'd find his child.

" 'Twas the old, oft-told sad story
  Of a woman's unbounded love,
A tale of cruel deception,
  Of a fiend that no tears could move.
At last she was left to wander
  Thousands of miles away
From her childhood home and loved ones,
  With no place her poor head to lay.

"But her father for years had sought her,
  Wondering where she could be
Till he suddenly came upon her
  'Mid those rocks that you all can see:
In the road through the thicket below them,
  He found her in deadly strife,
Trying to flee from the villain
  Who promised to make her his wife.

"The father in terror shouted,
  Then the fiend, in his rage and fear,
Leveled his pistol and fired,
  And the bullet—it struck me here."
Then the old man bared his bosom
  And a ghastly wound revealed;
His voice was becoming weaker,
  Like a drunken man he reeled.

Two miners then sprang beside him
   And seated him on the ground,
Then the jury and those about them
   Leaned forward to catch each sound.
"*I* am that poor girl's father,"
   The old man whispered in pain,
"And to save her I shot that monster,
   Or my child he would quick have slain.

"When he fell she grasped his pistol,
   And speeded for help away;
'Twas then that these miners saw her,
   Where the dead man's body lay.
I was there, but too weak to utter
   A word or a feeble cry,
But their hands could with ease have touched me
   As they silently passed me by."

Tom Scott then addressed the jury,
   He told them the case was clear,
And he turned to the weeping woman
   To conceal an uprising tear;
In his face there was just enough shadow
   To soften his bright blue eye,
In his voice there was just enough sadness
   To hint at a pain gone by.

"Is she guilty?" he asked the jury,
In tones that were soft and low,
But the answer came swift as lightning
In a thundering, mighty "No!"

The village is gone, and the actors—
God knows if one living there be;
And in Dead Man's Gulch so gloomy,
But one lonely grave you'll see.

Jaqueline.

Little Jaqueline sat 'neath an old oaken tree,
In a cool, shady dell, near the brink of a spring,
  And her pitcher lay empty beside her.
And her dark chestnut ringlets fell reckless and
      free
O'er her plump, dimpled shoulders, there seeming
      to cling
  As though jealous some ill might betide her;

While from under her hat beamed the loveliest
      eyes,
Of the tenderest, rarest and deepest of blue
  That kind Heaven e'er lavished on maiden.
Oh, what beauty revealed,—what a wealth to
      surmise,—
Thus encircled with wild flowers varied in hue,
  And the air with their scent richly laden.

It was witching to gaze on those round, faultless
      arms,   [her knee;
And the small, snowy hands that were clasped on
  She appeared such a fairy-like wee thing.
Yet no phantom was she, for her womanly charms
And her breast's undulations would make the
      doubt flee,
  And be proof that the creature was breathing.

(58)

In that lonely retreat, 'neath the old oaken tree,
Pretty Jaqueline lingered, still longing to stay,
  Though denying the reason she tarried.
She could do as she pleased, on that day she was
    free;
Yet she sighed as the moments stole swiftly
    away,
  For she knew on the next she'd be married.

Oh, the morning was bright, and the wedding
    was grand!
But the bride was too dull, and her face was so
    white;
  And then, why did her youthful voice falter?
For the groom's handsome features shone happy
    and bland.
Surely hearts of true lovers should swell with
    delight
  When they kneel before God's holy altar.

And the gossips, who seek only what we would
    hide,
Slyly hinted that naught but her hand had been
    won
  By the stranger's brief wooing and glitter.
For they thought of another than he at her side;
Of a love that in duty she ever must shun,
  Of a life that each vow would embitter.

In a calm, far away, on the Indian sea,
On the deck of a barque, sat a group of Jack tars
    Idly watching a seaman tattooing:
'Twas the arm of a landsman that lay on the knee
Of the indigo artist, and soon the blue scars
    Plainly told what the fellow was doing.

Only "Jaqueline"—hurriedly hid by his sleeve,
And the lubber strode off and gazed over the
    rail
    At the spars mirrored back by the ocean.
Such a warm heart and true, how could maiden
    deceive!
And he sighed as he stood there, dejected and
    pale,
    All alone with his hopeless devotion.

Twenty years have gone by. See that hollow-
    cheeked dame
Seated there, like a ghost, 'neath the globed
    chandelier
    With a fair, blooming damsel beside her!
That is Jaqueline; changed, quite, in all but the
    name.
She is rich, tho' her brilliant gems, flashing,
    appear
    By their splendor alone to deride her.

Poor mistaken; how sinful her secret regret!
And how vainly she tries to be loyal in thought
  To the man she has promised to cherish!
How she broods o'er one face that she ne'er can
    forget;
How in honor repelled and then eagerly sought
  The fond yearning that never can perish.

Then her child, the loved fetter that binds her to
    life,
How she dreads lest it meet with a fate like her
    own,
  And be bound, yet forever be parted!
There she sits, smiling down her soul's anguish
    and strife,
Seeking roses where briers and weeds have been
    sown;
  The proud mistress of wealth, — broken
  hearted.

If ye marry too soon, if ye marry too late,
Then beware of the curse, for the husband or
    wife
  May in time crave the love that was slighted.
Oh, the joy of the soul is in greeting its mate,
And the fullness of happiness dwells with that
    life
  Where the heart with the hand is united.

Music.

O music, gift beyond compare,
How oft thy beauties blessings bear!
How strong thy pow'r that binds to home
And bids the wayward cease to roam—
How sweet when wearied out with care
Some half forgot, familiar air!
The hearth-stone seems to brighter glow
When cheerful numbers gaily flow—
Good will, content and peace belong
Where music reigns with merry song.

The Potter's Field.

A gown of haze hung round the sleepy sun
As slowly down upon the hills he sank;
Soon, like a giant with full face, rubicund,
He paused, looked out upon the scene,
Then slipped beneath the quilts of purple gold
That lay in folds above his rocky couch.
The gauge of time had gone, for time is naught
To them that sleep; and nature ever wise
Ne'er gives a thing in vain: man's time is day.
Deep fell the shadows from the sombre trees
That fringed a flowing stream on either bank,
While weird and ghostly as a winding sheet
An ashy mist ascended slow.

(62)

Anon
Came forth the host nocturnal; wheeling bats,
The myriad swarm of insect life, the owl, and last
The stealthy quadruped.

Beside the stream
Looms up a withered yew, whose gaunt bare arms
No longer shelter give; and right beneath
The yew, there stands a hut, its sunken roof
And sides all crumbling with decay.   Within
The hut a candle's yellow glare falls full
Upon the wrinkled face of Haus Von Kraft.
His pipe, his jug of beer and pewter mug
Are there, as they have been each lonely night
For forty years; for forty years his hands
Have dug the graves that hold the city's dead—
The stranger, outcast, pauper, felon dead
From yon metropolis, whose many lights
Are shining bright against the sky.

Far off
A deep-toned bell booms out the hour, and Hans
Von Kraft arises slowly to his feet.
The old man peers into the dark without;
He takes his hat, his knotted staff, and strides
Adown the narrow path that leads to where
His silent wards are sleeping.   Now he stops,
For in the path where first begin the mounds
A human form disputes his way.   "Mein Gott!
Vot brings you here?" exclaims Von Kraft,

Who views with awe the outlines dim of that
Which stands before his bulging eyes. ''I come,''
Replies a hollow voice, ''to seek release
From this unhallowed ground.'' ''How comes
    you here?''   [look,
Asks Hans, in trembling tones. ''Sit there and
And hark, and you shall learn the cause that sent
Not only me, but all who fill these cells.''
Half wild with fright, old Hans, who knew not
    fear
Before this night, now drops upon his knees.
With awe-struck gaze and doubting brain he sees
From out each grave a head, a trunk, a corpse
Come forth, till every hillock holds a shape,
Some seated, some reclining, some erect,
But all intently looking at a ring of light,
A fleecy zone, like that which circles round
The moon when men predict a coming storm.
The tall, grim form which first he met now points
With bony finger at the light, the ring
Of glow-worm light, that hovers just above
The earth: he points, and sadly, solemnly
Explains: ''Behold, O man, this audience
Of dank and reeking death, each one of whom
Once shamed the virgin snow for purity;
Note well the cause that snapped the sacred tie,
That sent each heart adrift from virtue's realm,—
The first false step that ends in nameless woe.

Behold, for what you see in one lost life,
With equal truth and force applies to all
Who by that self-same cause were stricken low;
The difference of when and how is small,
When to a common foe a life succumbs:
He fell in battle, tells the tale; and though
By rifle, shell, or sabre thrust,
The death is justly charged to gory war.''

Now Hans Von Kraft is terrified indeed;
The Flying Dutchman, stories of the Rhine,
The olden legends of his Fatherland,
Are simple facts compared with what he sees;
The wildest things are true since this is true.
Look! look! a lovely scene appears
Within the ring phosphoric:
                          Happy home!
A father, mother, and their youthful son,
With merry guests surround a glowing hearth;
Content and peace have smoothed the frowns away
From every brow save one—and on her face,
The patient mother's face, a grief is stamped:
Her eyes speak out in mute appeal as he,
Her boy, accepts a proffered glass of wine
To drink his birthday toast.   He looks at her,
But laughs, and heeds her not.   Poor, foolish
        youth!
The home scene fades.

5

Now slowly dawns to view
Another, humbler home.   A pale young wife
Is seated by a cheerless grate.   A babe
Lies sleeping in a cradle at her side.
With wearied sigh the girlish mother turns
And looks upon the clock: it whirs, now strikes
The midnight hour.   O wretched life—how hope,
And doubt, and pain are flitting o'er
Her faded face!   She starts, she hears his
    step;
Her husband reels into the room and falls
Unconscious at her feet; she kneels beside
His form—the scene dies out.
             Old Hans Von Kraft
Attempts to rise—"No, no," vehement cries
The figure at his side, "you must not, shall
Not leave until you see the end!   That boy
I knew; I knew him as a man, I knew
Him as a wreck—O God, have mercy, look!"
And Hans, low stooping, looks.
              In bold relief,
Like chiseled statues stand a woman and
A child.   The circling rim of light makes plain
Each circumstance of feature, garb and form.
A tableau more than sad is this.   With hand
Outstretched the beggar mother pleads for help;
The little one half hides behind the rags
That barely hide the woman's form.   How wan,

How pinched their faces look! O Christ, what
    wrong
Have these two children wrought that they, like
    thou,
When thou wast here on earth, have not a place
To lay their heads!
           A hollow groan swells forth
In unison from every grave; the forms
Melt out—but only to give place to him
Whose weakness stole their strength away.
                   A man,
A weary tramp with bloated face, and eyes
All bleared with rum stands forth in grim despair.
The ring of light glows red; within grows black,
And on the black four words intensely burn:
The curse of drink.
          Half dazed old Hans Von Kraft
Now hears a wail of anguish wildly sad,
And shrieks and sobs; and now his spectre guest
Thus speaks: " 'Tis done. I said I knew that
    life—
Alas! Why should I not, for I am he!
Once loved—but now—ha! what is that I see?
O joy!"
        Within the ring a peaceful home
Again appears. An old man from the Book
Of God reads out; a gray haired dame sits near
The table whereon rests the book, and at

Her side a younger wife in widow's weeds,
While at the widow's feet a child reclines.
"Oh, do they think of me, and love me still?"
The goblin cries.   A scroll descends and hides
The group—upon it are these words in gold:

> Those once loved we love forever,
>   Still they come and go at will,
> For their mem'ries, like our shadows,
>   Haunt our steps through good or ill;
> Though the heart so freely trusted
>   False has proved or lost to sin,
> Yet we sigh and wish in sorrow
>   That the error had not been.

> Pride may mask the look of pity
>   That the willing soul would give,
> Anger thwart the heart's forgiveness,
>   Yet will Love immortal live:
> Night may hide the rose's beauty,
>   Storms her tender leaves may chill,
> But though hid, though cold and broken,
>   Must she shed her fragrance still.

Old Hans Von Kraft jumps up in fright and
        knocks
His pipe and jug of beer from off the bench;
He starts, and yawns, and rubs his eyes.

The night
Is far advanced, yet one such dream is quite
Enough—and so he lit his pipe and smoked
Till day.

A Sunset Ray.

The drooping rose may still some fragrance yield,
　The withering tree some shelter give,
The failing brook some moisture to the field,
　And dying, bless while yet they live.
Thus may I too, though broken-down and ill,
　Impart some goodness while I stay,
If only this fond duty to fulfill—
　To love and guard thee till I pass away.

The Felon's Wife.

The scene was a court of justice, where criminals
    were tried,
And a woman and child stood sobbing close by a
    prisoner's side.
The man was the woman's husband, the child
    their darling boy,
And they waited the dreadful sentence that would
    two fond lives destroy.
The sunshine streamed through the window and
    fell on the judge's face,
While the song of a bird in a tree-top seemed
    harsh and out of place;
Then the sunlight merged into shadow, and the
    bird had ceased to sing—
So quick are the fitful changes that fate and
    nature bring.

The ordeal soon was over, and the woman stood
    alone,
Alone with her tender offspring, with a heart
    that weighed like stone.
The convict's tear still glistened like a gem on
    her pallid cheek,
And that tear-drop mutely told her what his
    white lips could not speak.

'Twas a sad farewell, that parting, for it severed
man and wife—
Doomed her to toil unaided; him to servitude
for life:
But time soothes the deepest sorrow, and love
will hope and pray,
And soon like a dream grew the terrors of that
sad and awful day.

  *   *   *   *   *   *   *   *

'Tis night on the Mississippi, and a steamer,
staunch and new,
Has stopped at a village landing her fuel to
renew;
A man, the only passenger, steps hurriedly on
board,
And mates and crew stand ready, waiting the
captain's word:
"Haul in the gang-plank, lively! cast off your
hawser, quick!"
Who—oo! blows the hoarse, loud whistle, for the
fog hangs low and thick:
Dong! dong! rings the pilot's signal; plash!
plash! go the mammoth wheels,
And into the gloomy shadows, like a monster
swan she steals.

A hundred souls are sleeping, and the engine's
    throbbing drone
Has lulled the weary look-out with its drowsy
    monotone.
Now the mist is lifting slightly, and a light
    gleams on the shore—
'Tis gone; now the night grows blacker, more
    dismal than before:
Who—oo! goes the whistle hoarsely, but the
    steamer plows along,
For the pilot knows his bearings and he softly
    hums a song.
Who—oo! comes a sound, and faintly, like an
    echo far away;
And the engine still is droning, still is heard the
    raining spray:

"Boat ahead, sir!" calls the look-out; "Ay, ay,
    sir, boat ahead!"
Thus replies the watchful pilot as he glances at
    the red,
Then turns to see the green light, which the
    mist-clouds magnify
Till upon each wheelhouse, gleaming, stares a
    single monster eye.
Below the lights burn dimly, for all are locked
    in sleep,

Save the stewardess and a porter who silent vigil
    keep—
Who—oo! that's close upon us! dong! quick
    goes the pilot's bell,
The engineer springs promptly and handles his
    lever well:

"God help us! what has happened?" the frantic
    people cry,
While terror and wild confusion are seen in
    every eye:
Hark to the trampling overhead! to the rudder's
    rattling chain!
To the shrieks that come from the cabin, where
    the women still remain!
One blinding flash! one shudder! now every‐
    thing is still,
Save the swash of the flowing river, and the sigh
    of the night wind chill.
The papers were full of the story, 'twas their
    theme for a day or more,
Then the tale grew old and the world rolled on
    as smoothly as before.

In a lowly home by the river live a woman and
    her son,
And the lines on their patient faces show what
    toil and care have done:

They stand with a priest and surgeon, near the
    bed of a dying man,
And hark to his broken whispers, while his
    ashen face they scan:
His life had been worse than wasted, and his
    soul was black with sin,
And a seething hell of sorrow was raging his
    breast within—
"Yet—I'd—make—one—reparation—" and his
    trembling voice sinks low—
"I—would — do—one—thing—of — honor—tho'
    the last—before—I—go.

"From—the—wreck —of — the —smouldering—
    steamer—fate—bore—me—bleeding—here,—
That—my—awful—retribution— to—these—vic-
    tims—might—appear—
I—swear!—" and his voice grows louder, "if—
    you—search—that—satchel—there—
You—will —find—some—strange—confessions—
    and—the—proofs—of—truth—they bear—"
On the wall hangs a bag all blistered, which the
    woman hastes to reach,
For she of all his hearers knows the purport of
    his speech.
"This proves my husband's innocence! Thank
    God for what you've said!"

And she turns to the lonely passenger, only to
    find him dead.

   *   *   *   *   *   *   *   *

Softly the sunbeams golden steal by a prison bar,
Lighting an empty dungeon whose iron door
    stands ajar;
And the same sun lights a cottage, with a warm
    and cheery glow,
Where three fond hearts united, with rapture
    overflow:
"O husband," the woman whispers, "I knew
    that you told me true;"
And he smiles and gently answers, "Let us our
    vows renew;
Come, boy, kiss your new found mother, whom
    we'll love to the end of life,
For we've bid farewell forever to the grief-tried
    felon's wife."

The Four Kisses.

A baby on a woman's breast
Has fallen asleep in peaceful rest;
With tender care she lays it down,
Draws o'er its feet the tiny gown;
Then, thrilled with love, with holy bliss,
Bends low and gives
                    A mother's kiss.

With blushing cheeks, with downcast eyes
A maiden struggles, softly sighs,
Then yields.   And from her fancy's flow
Drinks deep the joy that angels know;
Thus two hearts learn the rapturous bliss
That comes to all, with
                    Love's first kiss.

A troop halts at a cottage door,
A young wife craves one moment more;
Her husband draws her to his side,
"Thou art," says he, "a soldier's bride;
O love, I can but give thee this—
And this—and this—
                    My farewell kiss."

(76)

The lamps shed forth a tender light
Upon a sweet face, cold and white;
The flowers lie strewn, the dirge is sung,
The rite is o'er, the bell has rung:
God help them, by that dread abyss,
Who sobbing press
    The last sad kiss.

The Dead Letter.

There, now! I've read your letter through
   Three times; I'll read it once again
If you say so; it rests with you.
   What? loan you paper, ink and pen?
Why, man, you're weaker than a child.
   To-morrow I will gladly write
Whate'er you wish. Be reconciled,
   Compose yourself and rest to-night.

You think we nuns are good to tend
   The sick, to count our beads, and pray,
But that we do not comprehend
   How worldly people dread delay
In getting word from those they love:
   Why, sir, you know not what you say—
Ah! this dark robe too well doth prove
   The sorrow of that by-gone day—

No, no; I fully understand
   What you would say. There's no offence;
Naught to forgive. There take my hand.
   We now are friends. In confidence
The story of a broken life,
   Before the doctor comes, I'll tell:
Of how I shunned the cold world's strife
   And sought a quiet convent cell.

(78)

Far back in life I loved a man,
  A gen'rous, noble heart and true:
And he loved me as only can,
  As only gallant natures do.
Our days passed by so quietly,
  Love's dream so rosy-hued had grown
That seasons glided by ere we
  Would note that e'en a month had flown.

Thus ran my girlhood and his youth,
  Till came the naming of the happy day—
Our wedding day—that would in truth
  Have made us man and wife for aye,
When, like a blow from one we love,
  There came an unexpected woe;
In vain 'gainst fate we madly strove;
  Each cherished hope lay scattered low.

A crime had been committed in
  The village where lived he and I;
And 'mid the first wild, senseless din
  That marked the people's hue and cry,
Suspicion on him fell, and so,
  To 'scape the frenzied, 'vengeful mob,
He, innocent, resolved to go
  Away—and I to stay and sob.

Then, bending low, said he, "This thing
   Will only for a season last,
A moment full relief may bring;
   At most our grief will soon be past;
But, darling, should it not be so,
   Write" (he whispered a fictitious name),
"And I will by your letter know
   That in your eyes I bear no shame."

The rain fell from a dark'ning sky,
   The apple blossoms scattered lay,
The chill wind moaned, and night drew nigh,
   As with a sigh he turned away—
I watched his form till lost in gloom,
   And, save the dripping of the rain,
There fell a stillness of the tomb—
   A lull that seemed to daze my brain.

The morning after that sad night
   The guilty one was found; and I,
With woman's haste, sat down to write,
   And wrote in joyous ecstasy;
The letter mailed, each moment seemed
   An age; but days and weeks passed by—
With visions dread my fancy teemed—
   But came he not, nor made reply.

One day, when hope had almost fled,
  The postman thrust it in my hand:
"This is from Washington," he said,
  "Dead-letter office, understand?"
With throbbing heart I broke the seal,
  My face grew whiter than a sheet,
The dreadful blunder made me reel
  And drop the letter at my feet.

Instead of the fictitious name
  He gave, it bore his own,
Which knowing not, he could not claim—
  To him my lines were never known—
In loneliness he died: and here
  I nurse the sick; but I have done—
And, sir, no longer have a fear
  To trust me, though I'm but a nun.

You've heard a portion of my tale
  Before? From whom? Oh, tell me quick!
From my lost love? You both set sail
  In the same ship? My heart grows sick—
What? Still alive? Oh, God be praised!
  Oh, joy! Oh, joy! And I will write?
Now that my dead to life is raised—
  Will I? Yes, now—this very night.

The Coquette.

Two girls sat in a gay saloon, nor mingled with
    the crowd;
The younger's face was pale and sad, the elder's
    stern and proud.

"Oh, Gertrude," said the younger girl, "thou
    art a sad coquette;
Ah, many hearts have felt thy power, and thou
    art flirting yet.

"There's one who fills a foreign grave, who loved
    thee all too well,
Who breathed thy name forgivingly as in the
    fray he fell;

"And yet his fate was better far than that of
    poor Martelle,
Who lonely clanks his heavy chains—a mad-
    man—in his cell.

"Oh, Gertrude," in a softer tone, "give up thy
    selfish arts,
Or hopeless love will be thy doom for blighting
    loving hearts."

Thus far had Maud unchecked reproved, when
    Gertrude coldly said,
"I care not for the living dupes, why blame me
    for the dead?

"Thy lover, sure, is naught to me, so quell thy
    jealous fears;
When seeking game I ever strive to strike among
    my peers."

"'Tis not my lover," Maud replied, while
    blushes bathed her brow,
"But brother Paul I fain would save—for him
    I'm pleading now.

"Of kin, he's all I have on earth—so noble,
    brave and pure—
Too good, alas, to sacrifice—defeat he'd ne'er
    endure."

But Gertrude rose and took the hand that claimed
    her for the dance,
While Maud stole to the balcony—did Paul stand
    there by chance?

It seemed not so—anon there came a lass sur-
    passing fair;
Some hurried words, a merry laugh—they seek
    the gaslight's glare.

Soon Paul claims Gertrude for the waltz; she
    yields and softly sighs,
Then off they whirl while glances dart from
    scores of jealous eyes.

    *   *   *   *   *   *   *   *

The full round moon now rides on high; the
    fragrant air is cool,
The fountain's spray, like flashing gems, darts
    in the limpid pool.

A rustic seat girts round an oak, and Paul leads
    Gertrude there,
She by his side, he takes her hand, so small, so
    soft and fair.

In accents low he thus began: "Oh, Gertrude, till
    to-night
True happiness I never knew, and may it ne'er
    take flight.

"Say, may I tell my tale, and hope to gain a
    smile from thee?
Approving words to ease a heart that is no longer
    free?

"I'm lonely now, for sister Maud is soon to be a
    bride;
Then wonder not because I seek a refuge at thy
    side."

She murmured half inaudibly: "Dear Paul, I
    long to hear;
Thou'lt get a smile for ev'ry smile, a tear for
    ev'ry tear."

"Enough, kind Gertrude, listen then: for years
    I've roamed afar;
I've sailed beneath the Southern Cross, I've lost
    the Northern Star;

"But now I once more breathe the air of home,
    I'll never stray;
I only need a loving wife—why tremble, Ger-
    trude, say?

"But soon I'll tell thee all I may; say, wilt thou
    share my joy?
God willing, this night, two weeks hence, I
    marry Kate LeRoy."

Poor Gertrude heard no more that eve, nor saw
    she Paul again;
The rose-tints faded from her cheeks; at last she
    loved—in vain.

      *   *   *   *   *   *   *   *

Her wasted form the church-yard holds; Ah!
    never this forget:
A woman's love is woman's life, e'en tho' a gay
    coquette.

Six O'Clock.

Down by the rugged coast of Maine
Breaks on the air the glad refrain
That welcomes old Time on his westward flight,
That makes the dull eye of the toiler bright,
And heralds the bliss of a single night;
Thus bell and whistle with clang and shriek,
At six o'clock, and six times a week.

Loveliest hour of all the day,
Blest is thy sweet and mystic sway:
Affection and hope in their might are rife
In each watching child; in the waiting wife;
The father that tramps from his daily strife;
The widow's son and his fond embrace;
In the smile that beams on her pallid face.

Who hath not felt the wondrous spell,
Ushered by whistle and by bell?
A halo of peace round each home it flings;
To poor and to weary relief it brings;
And e'en the black tea-kettle gaily sings:
O moments calm! Ye foretell the rest
That soon must come to each human breast.

Westward speed on o'er hill and dell,
City and town and cot to tell;

(86)

On, on, like a courier, dash away,
Hard pressing the heels of departing day
Till stopped by the waters of " 'Frisco" Bay!
Thus bell and whistle with clang and shriek,
At six o'clock, and six times a week.

True Friendship.

'Twixt friends there is a silken tie
That binds, unseen, 'neath sunlit sky,
When hearts are gay and bright the eye,
  When pleasure's words are spoken;
But when comes grief, distress and pain,
Behold the silken tie's a chain
Whose links ill fortune strikes in vain
  And sorrow leaves unbroken.

The Sailor's Story.

Flood tide. "All strangers leave the ship!"
  The boatswain hoarsely cried.
Then hand grasped hand in fervent grip,
And lips pressed lips in fond adieu,
  As o'er the vessel's side
Each loved one parted from her crew.

"Dear mother," keep this flageolet
  Till I come home from sea—
I'll often write, nor shall forget
I am a widow's only stay—
  God bless you, pray for me,
Be quick! the vessel's under weigh!"

The ship sailed off. The sailor boy,
  That woman's darling child,
So late her sad life's only joy,
Soon grew to like his new friends' ways,
  To join their revels wild—
While lone his mother passed her days.

In far-off lands he learned to love
  The soul-distressing cup,
Nor ever sought for help above;
Home, mother, God, all were forgot,
  Good thoughts rum swallowed up
And left him but a helpless sot.

(88)

At home, his mother, bent and wan,
   Toils patient day and night,
Oft bending o'er her work till dawn;
And oft against the window pressed
   Her face is seen, a sight
Most touching, careworn, grief-distressed.

The letter-man has passed the door,
   He does so ev'ry day;
The widow's heart is sick and sore,
For not a line in three long years
   Has come to light her way
Or stop the flowing of her tears.

By piecemeal all her scanty store
   Has gone to buy her bread,
Yet sickness, want, claim one thing more,
The thing she fain would cling to yet,
   And fainting, almost dead,
She pawns her darling's flageolet.

The awnings flap, the shutters bang,
   The night air's filled with sleet;
Three golden balls above us hang,
Below, a woman, stiff and cold,
   Lies, friendless, in the street—
Dead, near the flageolet she sold!

A broker's sale.   The room is filled
  (For Christmas time is near)
With some to buy, while others chilled
Have slipped in from the biting cold.
  "We want a bid, look here,
Silver-keyed, and washed with gold!"'

The auctioneer then paused, for, lo!
  A man leaped on his stand,
"My flageolet! oh, mother's woe!"'
And sobs choked up the sailor's throat,
  As with his brawny hand
His heaving bosom wild he smote.

He learned, though late, that wine deceives,
  That strong drink leads to death;
That abstinence alone relieves
The drunkard from disgrace, distress,
  Makes pure his rum-fouled breath,
That temperance doth ever bless.

And thus the sailor's story ends,
  A story all too true;
Yet judge not harshly, gentle friends,
He was a loving boy and brave,
  Loved by a reckless crew,
Whose lesson is a mother's grave.

The Old Spinster.

No, she never was married, but was to have
    been—
    At the time she was running the loom—
But the fact'ry burned down, some were mangled
    and scarred,
    And her lover was never her groom,
As he wedded a handsomer girl.

To the stranger, old Rachel was ugly indeed,
    For her features were grim and distorted;
Tho' in years long gone by she was lovely and
    fair,
    As the hopes of her life that were thwarted
By the dreadful mishap in the mill.

But beneath the plain calico gown that she wore,
    Beat a heart that was loving and tender—
As the villagers knew—and man, woman or child
    'Gainst the merest rude speech would defend
    her,
So well was the poor woman loved.

And right many's the maid, who, bewailing her
    woe,
    Has told Rachel the slight that distressed her,
Only soon to trip on with a happier look,
    While the silly goose inwardly blessed her,
For her comforting words and advice.

Then the urchins have gone to her, covered with
    mud,
  Afraid to go home—perhaps crying—
But old Rachel (the remedy) washed out the
    stains,
  And they laughed while their garments were
    drying,
In the yard at the back of her cot.

When the villagers slept, and the cricket and owl,
  And the rustling of leaves were unheeded,
In the room of the sick, by the flickering light
  Was she seen, where her presence was needed,
While her gaunt shadow danced on the wall.

And the outcasts who begged at her door for a
    crust,
  Ere they went on their wearisome ways,
Felt that one thought them human and pitied
    their fate,
  Who recalled the remembrance of earlier days,
And who reckoned them not by their rags.

But the weight of her grief which was never
    revealed,—
  Save to Jesus—the friend of the lowly—
Bore her down—and the sands of her desolate
    life,
  Which for years had been ebbing out slowly,
Ceased to run—and her spirit was freed.

When the villagers stood at the side of her grave,
 When the gray-headed preacher's voice fal-
  tered,
When the tears trickled down the bronzed cheeks
 of the men—
 Oh! her beauty seemed fresh and unaltered
As when happy she worked in the mill.

And oft where she lies a bent form can be seen
 When the twilight is deep'ning its shadows:
And the sweetest of flow'rets are found on her
 tomb,
 All fresh from the dew-gleaming meadows;
Yet who gathers them no one can tell.

The Deacon's Sermon.

Mortal man is prone to blunder,
   So is mortal woman, too;
Any one is apt to blunder,
   I am apt to, so are you.

But the blunder of all blunders,
   That will blunder be for life,
Is when choosing to make blunder
   In a husband or a wife.

Marriages, they say, are destined,
   Made by wiser powers on high;
But for that no proof is shown us,
   Nor is given a reason why.

If your idol short or tall is,
   Silken tressed, or bald, or gray,
Fair and youthful, old and wrinkled,
   Sad in look, or bright and gay,—

If both talented and wealthy,
   If unlettered, humble, poor,
This remember: If love guides you
   All things else you may endure.

Dying to Win.

Fierce blows the gale and cold,
  Loudly the windows rattle;
Why, the stars seemed never half so bright.
Hark! 'Twas a bell that tolled—
  There, again! must I battle
Through another dreadful winter night?

Better by far to die.
  Who in this mighty city
Wastes a thought on such a wretched life?
Who heeds my weary sigh?
  Who sheds a tear in pity?
All alone I wage the bitter strife.

Bright gleams yon chandelier,
  Gay sound the reckless voices;
And how tempting warm the red grate glows!
No! rather perish here—
  Ah, no—my soul rejoices,
For I triumph spite of all my woes.

Now, that I've made my vow,
  Who comes to help me keep it?
Are the saints that preach asleep or dead?
Ripe is the harvest now,
  Yet comes there none to reap it.
Not a cent! no home; no crust of bread.

(95)

Fie, upon hearts so cold!
  Not one will deign to aid me;
And my own sex turn me off with scorn;
Sneer at me; call me bold;
  Taunt me, and then upbraid me—
Oh, my God, how can I wait till morn?

Mother, is that you there?
  Surely, I must be dreaming—
Do not leave me, mother; take me home!
Oh, how keen bites the air!
  Yonder the dawn is gleaming.
It is I, your child: Oh, mother, come!

Sleepy, indeed, am I—
  Wait till I kneel down, mother—
Now I lay me down to sleep—keep off—
Help! help! help! I shall die—
  Give me some air—I smother!
I am saved!   Now let the cold world scoff.

*   *   *   *   *   *   *

Fierce blows the gale and cold,
  Loudly the windows rattle,
And the stars are paling out with fright:
Oh, 'tis a tale oft told:
  Done is the hard-fought battle—
And a weary soul has said good-night.

A Legend of the Declaration.

A hundred years and more have fled
  Since brave Columbia burst the chains
That tyranny and avarice wed.
Then liberty was yet a dream—
  A hymn still sung in whispered strains—
A first gray dawn, a herald beam
    Of Freedom's sun.

'Twas then oppression's ruthless hand
  Was striving to regain its prey,
And spread dismay throughout the land.
Heroic souls at once convened
  To crush a hated monarch's sway,
Whose dastard rule had fully weaned
    His subjects' love.

Each colony her chosen sent
  To Philadelphia's spacious hall,
The people's will to represent.
Success would crown them Patriots brave—
  One thing was needful to them all,
Or each might find a traitor's grave—
    'Twas unanimity.

The Continental Congress met;
  Each delegate had said his say,
Save one, who had not spoken yet.
With us the vote remained a tie:
  Good Pennsylvania held the sway—*
'Twas she who now must cast the die,
      To wreck or save.

John Morton's called; all eyes are strained—
  The Federal Arch is almost built—
The arch that Freedom's God ordained.
He voted right, all undismayed
  E'en though his true heart's blood be spilt—
And thus he nobly, safely laid
      The Keystone.

And so the mighty deed was done,
  That makes us what we are to-day,
By which our sovereign right was won.
John Morton gained eternal fame,
  'Twill last with Independence day,
And Pennsylvania gained a name—
      The Keystone State.

  * The vote on the Declaration was by Colonies. Six had voted
for and six against the measure; the Pennsylvania delegation
had the casting vote, and it being equally divided, John Morton
decided the momentous question, thus making Pennsylvania the
"Keystone State."

The River.

The sun had set. The ruddy clouds
  Had changed to gloomy gray,
And sweet, sad twilight soothed the hour
  Forsaken by the day.

A village road, with nest-like cots,
  And oaks, on either hand.
An old stone bridge, whose single arch,
  A dark, deep river spanned:

And sounds of distant merry shouts
  Were borne upon the breeze,
When, on the bridge there came a maid
  And sank upon her knees.

A maid? Perhaps a slighted wife—
  Or neither—none could tell—
A stricken life—a broken heart,
  About to bid farewell—

Farewell to that, which lacking hope,
  Is but a dreary waste;
Where Nature's brightest, fairest sweets
  Grow bitter to the taste.

She rose—advanced unto the brink—
    A wild, imploring prayer—
Alas! she stood, unloved—alone—
    A statue of despair.

One plaintive wail, and then a plunge—
    The wavelets laved the shore—
Then all was still.   The river flowed
    As smoothly as before.

A Grain of Truth.

The luxury derived in doing good
Is oft the only recompense men get
For kindly deeds; e'en toil of years is paid
Too oft with ingrate acts, and motives pure
As angel thoughts are powerless to stay
Suspicion's tongue; but, oh, 'tis sweet to know
Our duty has been done 'twixt man and man,
To feel we have been loyal to ourselves;
To know one voice at least proclaims us true,
The whispered voice of God, within our hearts!

Out of Season.

The breakers sing the same old song
 As in the days of yore,
And the sea-birds skim the surf along
 As gayly as before;
But the lighthouse looms above the fell,
 Like the over-tired ghost
Of some poor, lonely sentinel
 Forgotten on his post.
No footprints mark the gleaming sands,
Nor puddles, made by tiny hands,
But drear and barren slopes the beach
To where the rushing billows reach.

The wreck whose rotten ribs and dank
 Are bedded in the strand,
That marks the place the swimmer sank
 While drifting from the land—
In the days agone a trysting place,
 Where the fond love vows were said—
Now seems to clasp in weird embrace
 Its ancient, gallant dead.
The ebb and flow of the salty tide,
 The crash of the tumbling wave,
So constant, mock the love that died,
 The sailor's shifting grave.

No more the merry voice is heard,
  The jest, or repartee,
The vulgar shout, nor friendly word
  Nor chant of passing glee.
And the old board-walk gives forth no sound,
  For the feet that here once trod
Are pressing other, distant ground,
  Or resting 'neath the sod.
A gray-beard, mule, and crazy cart
  Move down the noble drive,
Of summer's busy scenes a part,
  That lonely still survives.

How like a city of the dead,
  Plague-struck, or seared by fate—
How all the life and mirth have fled,
  How drear and desolate!
The lofty structure, cozy cot,
  And the broad and lengthy porch,
Where dozed the throng all limp and hot,
  Or strolled to 'scape the summer's scorch;
The halls, where maiden, beau and bride
  Oft danced 'mid music and garlands grand
The waltz, quadrille and graceful glide—
  Alike deserted, mournful stand!

The twilight fades, the crescent dips
  Low down the western sky,
The shadow-forms of distant ships
  Are lost unto the eye;

Yet the mystic voice of the ocean old
    Finds an echo in the heart,
And lulled is the breast of the meek or bold
    At the tales the waves impart;
The lofty mountain thrills the soul,
    And pleasant is the lea,
But peace reigns where the billows roll—
    'Tis whispered by the sea!

A Lover's Wish.

Thou hast a place within my heart
Where others ne'er can share a part—
There thou alone, with power serene,
Shall ever reign, my chosen queen:
'Mid all the scenes of busy life,
When wearied out with worldly strife,
At twilight gray, at midnight drear,
Thy lovely form seems ever near.

O Fate, forbid that love like this
Should never know a sweeter bliss
Than that which only dreams accord,
Or hope, desire and faith afford!
I crave with all my soul that thine
May wed eternally with mine—
And not in name, but heart and life,
That thou wilt be my cherished wife.

Woman.

You ask what I think of woman,
    If I deem her nature true,
Or think her a creature fickle
    That the wise should not pursue.
You ask for my frank opinion
    Of her heart's uncertain laws,
As judged by the scribes and poets
    In their thousand time-worn saws.
Well, I'll give you the information,
    Only glad to know I can,
For men may, perhaps, believe it,
    Since the witness is a man.

All women are pure by instinct,
    As the lily at birth is white;
And as northward points the needle,
    So their souls incline to right.
Woman's ever first in goodness,
    First in pity, first to bless,
And when scorned, deceived or tempted,
    Last, reluctant, to transgress.
Her faith in reciprocation
    Is the chain that binds her love—
In that dream her heart's as steadfast
    As the stars that burn above.

(104)

Rizpah.

2 Samuel xxi. 1-11.

Night came at last.   The noisy throng had gone,
And where the sun so late, like alchemist,
Turned spear and shield and chariot to gold
No sound was heard.

              The awful deed was done;
And vengeance sated to the full had turned
Away.   The Amorites had drunk the blood
Of Saul and were content.   The last armed guard
Had gone, and stillness dwelt upon the scene.
The rocky mount slept fast in solitude;
The dry, dead shrubs stood weird and grim, and
     marked
The narrow, heated road that sloped and wound
To join the King's highway.   No living thing
Was seen; nor insect, bird nor beast was heard;
The very air came noiselessly across
The blighted barley fields below, yet stirred
No leaflet with its sultry breath.

                    Above,
A mist half hid the vaulted firmament,
And stars shone dimly as though through a veil;
Still was their light full adequate to show
Those rigid shapes that seeming stood erect,
Yet bleeding hung, each from its upright cross,
A mute companion to its ghastly kin.

The middle watch was come, yet silence still
Oppressed the night; the twigs stood motionless
Like listening phantoms, 'when, from out
The shadow of a jutting rock there came
A moving thing of life, a wolf-like form:
With slow and stealthy tread it came, then
    stopped
To sniff the air, then nearer moved to where
The seven gibbets stood.
                 Then came a shriek,
A cry of mortal fear that pierced the soul
Of night; then up from earth a figure sprang,
The frightened jackal leaped away, and once
More Rizpah crouched beneath her dead.
                     So night
And day she watched; beneath the burning sun
By day, beneath the stars and moon by night;
All through the long Passover Feast she watched.
Oft in the lonely vigil back through years
She went; in fancy she was young again,
The favored one of mighty Saul, the King;
Again she mingled with the courtly throng,
And led her laughing boys before her lord,
Their father.
          Starting then, with upturned face,
And gazing from her hollow, tearless eyes,
Her blackened lips would move, but make no
    sound,

Then sinking to the ground she caught once
    more
The thread of thought, and thought brought
    other scenes;
She saw the stripling warrior David, son
Of Jesse, whom the populace adored
And Saul despised; then Merab came, and then
Her sweet-faced sister, Michal, whose quick wit
And love saved David's life.
                Then Rizpah rose,
Yea, like a tigress sprang unto her feet.
"Thou David, curst be thee and thine!" she
    shrieked,
"Thou ingrate murderer! Had Saul but lived,
And hadst thou fallen upon thy sword instead,
My sons, my children still would live!"
                     'Twas in
The morning watch, and Rizpah's last, that
    bright,
Clear glowed the Milky Way. The Pleiades
Like molten gold shone forth; e'en she who loved
The mortal Sisyphus peeped timidly,
And so the Seven wond'ring sisters gazed
Upon the Seven crucified below.
Such cause for woman's pity ne'er was seen,
And stars, e'en stones might weep for Rizpah's
    woe,
Whose mother-love was deathless as her soul.

The gray dawn came. The sky was overcast;
The wind had changed, and sobbed a requiem.
Still Rizpah slept, and dreamed. She heard the
    sound
Of harps and timbrels in her girlhood home—
When rush of wings awakened her. She rose,
Her chilled form shaking unto death. She looked,
And saw the loathsome vultures at their work.
With javelin staff in hand she beat them off,
But bolder were they as she weaker grew,
Till one huge bird swooped at her fierce,
And sunk its talons in her wasted arm.
She threw it off, the hideous monster fled,
And Rizpah fell. It then began to rain.
The famine ceased, and Rizpah's watch was done.

Lines to Lizzie—1866.

Had I but thy sweet face to cheer my way
The darkest night would seem as bright as day;
No earthly cares could mar my happy lot,
The dreary past should ever be forgot:
Nor could I wish for more, nor ask for less
When rev'ling in such perfect happiness;
For, to man, is woman not truly worth
Just what the sun is to our own cold earth?

Farewell.

With white sails set the vessels glide
Fast onward o'er the drifting tide.
'Tis now while near and yet in view
That still is heard the fond adieu;
'Tis now that lips and gestures tell
The heart's good-bye, the sad farewell!

To-night, when sails to sight are lost
And gloomy darkness veils the coast;
To-night, when children fast asleep
Forget who sails the lonely deep,
To one will sound, like funeral knell,
Her husband's dreaded word, farewell.

The helmsman, as he grasps the wheel,
The sea spray on his cheek can feel,
And to his mind each drop appears
The moisture of his loved ones' tears;
And in a song he tries to quell
The sadness of their sweet farewell.

Each day the word "Farewell" is said,
The silent, parting tear is shed;
And so each day warm hearts unite,
Some home is reached, some eye made bright;
What glooms the word is: none can tell
Which time 'twill be a last farewell.

The Caliph's Dream.

I stood alone beside a mighty sea;
The waves in awful majesty swept in
And crashed upon the strand.   Far out beyond
The snowy-crested line of breakers rode
A ship; and as she rose and fell her tall
Masts seemed to trace a message on the sky:
"O ship! O restless waste!" I cried, "Be true,
Be merciful, that they who watch on board,
And they that wait at home, may once more
    clasp
The hands and press the lips of those they love."

The vision changed.   I sat beneath my tent.
'Twas noon.   Upon my right the desert sands
Stretched hot and gleaming till they touched the
    sky;
Upon my left lay leagues of sand; before,
Behind; which way I looked was burning sand:
The fierce sun overhead poured down a stream
Of heat intolerable.   Silence reigned.
The caravan had gone.   I leaned low down
To hearken, but in vain.   Abandoned!   Lost!
Would my siesta prove a sleep of death?

Another scene: The sun had set, and peace
Pervaded hill and dale.   A sweet perfume   .

Of flowers filled the evening air. The sound
Of tinkling bells came faintly from a plain
Where camels browsed. The slender minarets,
And stately domes of mosques, proclaimed a
     town,
That nestled 'mid the distant, waving palms.
A troop of horsemen slowly came in view;
Their banner bore the crescent and the star.
I knelt and cried: "Praise be to Allah's name!"

And then, it seemed, I was within a grot
That opened on a placid lake. The moon
Was at the full and o'er the water threw
A track of silver sheen. Beside me stood
A child with upturned face. I placed my hand
Upon its head, when, lo! from out the lake
Arose a horrid, monster form. It glared
With baleful eyes and then advanced. "Keep
     off!
Keep off!" I shrieked, then seized the child and
     turned
To fly—when suddenly the vision changed:

Once more I dwelt beneath my parents' roof,
A happy, careless child. The olden scenes
Were fresh again, and things forgot had life
And form. O home!—how blest are they that
     have
A home!—sweet haven sure when others fail!

"Oh, do not leave me, darling boy, my own!"
It was my mother's voice.   Ah, yes, her eyes
Were beaming love, as angel-like she smiled
And kissed my brow.   And, as I watched her
       face,
I woke and wept to know 'twas but a dream.

Woman's Worth.

I still maintain that woman
    Alone lends charm to life,
That for her smile approving
    Man braves all toil and strife;
Without her, earth were empty,
    Its pathways drear and long,
Its harvests gloomy banquets
    Devoid of mirth and song.

Kindly Acts.

A kindly act is seldom lost,
And, oh, how small indeed the cost,
That oft relieves the breast of pain,
And bids the heart take hope again!

The Burning City.

Fire! Fire! Hark to the cry,
As the flames light up the lurid sky!
The hissing, the crackling, the dreadful roar—
The red tongues lapping the house tops o'er.
To the north! to the east! like a moving hell—
Shrieking and groaning—plunging pell-mell,
Madly the withering demon comes!
Leaving his trail in the smould'ring homes,
In the shrunken, black, disfigured corse—
Invalid, infant, dog and horse
Alike they lay—while far ahead,
Where the terror-stricken throng have fled,
Bravely cov'ring the wild retreat
With their engines snorting in ev'ry street,
Or charging the foe with axe in hand,
The noble firemen make a stand—
Till wounded, blistered, wearied out,
They slowly join the gen'ral rout!
A motley medley, stricken with woe,
The houseless thousands onward go—
Packed like mules—some curse and rave,
Staggering under the goods they'd save;
A wailing babe, but partly dressed,
Nestles close to its father's breast,

8   (113)

While to his arm the pale-faced wife
Clings as though for her very life!
Barrows, wagons, carts and drays
Rumble away from the hungry blaze—
The sick take rest, and are left behind
To care for the lame, the weak and blind.
Murdering, pillaging—drunken yells!
And so the ghastly chorus swells,
Till morning breaks in the eastern sky,
And shows to the heavy, bloodshot eye,
Ruined Chicago!

Camellia.

Oh tell me why those drooping eyes
    Have lost their wonted light?
Eyes that ever were so cheerful,
Now so often sad and tearful,
    Mourning o'er some hidden blight—
Tell me why those weary sighs?

Has some fond hope cruelly broken
    Into fragments of despair—
Has some dream of sweet conception
Been dispelled by base deception,
    Or the thing deemed pure and fair
Proved a false and worthless token?

The Last Salute.

Yes, the ranks are growing smaller
  With the coming of each May,
And the beards and locks once raven
  Now are mingled thick with gray;
Soon the hands that strew the flowers
  Will be folded still and cold,
And our story of devotion
  Will forever have been told.

Years and years have passed by, comrades,
  Though it seems but yesterday
Since the Blue-garbed Northern legions
  Marched to meet the Southern Gray—
But a day since Massachusetts
  Bade her soldier boys good-bye—
But a day since Alabama
  Heard her brave sons' farewell cry.

Those are days we all remember,
  In our hearts we hold them yet;
And the kiss we got at parting,
  Who can ever that forget?
And it may have been a mother,
  A fond father, or a wife,
Or a maid whose love was dearer
  To the soldier's heart than life.

Then the silent midnight marches,
    And the fierce-fought battle's roar,
And the sailor's lonely watches,
    Gone, please God, forevermore:
Though these ne'er can be forgotten
    While the dew our graves shall wet,
Yet the color of our jackets
    Let each gallant heart forget;

For the ranks are growing smaller,
    And though decked in blue or gray,
Soon both armies will be sleeping
    In their shelter-tents of clay.
But the loud reverberation
    Of the last salute shall be
Oft re-echoed through the ages
    As the tocsin of the free!

For we both but did our duty,
    In the Great Jehovah's plan,
And the world has learned a lesson
    That all men may read who can;
And when gathered for the muster
    On the last and dreadful day,
May that God extend His mercy
    Sweet, alike to Blue and Gray.

The Pilgrim.

When alone by the banks of the river I stray
And watch the dark tide as it ripples away;
When I see the frail flow'rets of summer decay,
Which come with the morn and decline with the
     day—

When a meteor tracks its bright way through
     the sky,
Sheds forth its refulgence, then fades to the eye;
When the dead leaves of autumn are borne
     sadly by
On the winds as they hurry along with a sigh;

When I think of my childhood, that season of
     bliss,
And compare its fond joys with the sorrows of
     this;
When I strive to be true, yet in truth am remiss,
And stand on the brink of some sinful abyss—

When I trace in the embers one dearly loved
     face,
And dwell on the kiss and the farewell em-
     brace;

(117)

When I think of one form, of its beauty and
    grace,
Of the warm heart now cold in its last resting
    place—

Oh, how can I help, as I wearily plod,
A sigh for escape from the chastening rod,
When 'neath the blue violets, under the sod,
The highway leads on to a merciful God!

The Blessing of Sight.

As music thrills the soul with ecstasy
Although its essence is impalpable
As air; as perfumes sweet intoxicate
With force invisible, so many things
Unseen impart some pleasure to the mind,
Each like a melody: but yonder star,
The silent eloquence of yonder star
O'erwhelms me with a higher, nobler joy,
For in its golden fire I see the hand
Of God, the Master hand, whose mystic touch
Blends ev'ry bliss in one grand harmony.
How precious, then, the priceless boon of sight!

Approaching Spring.

Spring is coming; genial sunshine
   Soon will make the meadows green,
Fill the leafless boughs with foliage,
   Gladden all this dreary scene.
Soon the buttercups and daisies
   Will succeed the melting snow,
And the April showers urge the
   Stubborn mountain drifts to go.

Soon the frog will croak a greeting
   To his namesake on the tree,
While the evening hum of insects
   And the murmur of the sea
Blend in music low, and sweeter
   Than the choicest strains of art—
Nature's soft and plaintive whisp'rings
   Ever soothe the weary heart.

Countless songs in happy numbers
   Yearly greet the coming May;
Yet her brightness seems the brightness
   Of a sad October day
To the souls that Fate has frozen
   In the depths of bitter woe—
And the warbler's voice but mocks the
   Hidden griefs we may not show.

The Thief on the Cross.

ARGUMENT.

In order to portray the bold, defiant nature of the thief, he is first presented to the reader while lying in wait for a traveler, whom he attacks; during the combat the traveler momentarily gains the mastery, and the thief's life is threatened. Yet he scorns to plead for mercy, but, with a sudden effort, overpowers the traveler, whom he robs and leaves by the wayside. Again he is discovered in prison. It is the day of execution, just prior to the dread march to Calvary; here once more he shows an indomitable spirit, proud to the very death. The final scene is upon the cross, where, witnessing the sufferings and marvelous magnanimity of the dying Christ, he at last succumbs to the mighty power of love.

Crouching low, but not with fear,
A robber earthward bends his ear;
The distant footfalls nearer grow—
Hesitating, stumbling, slow;
Then quicker, as the 'lated wight
Beholds each cheerful, twinkling light;
Jerusalem lies at his feet,
Anon he'll tread the lively street;
Soon Olivet will be descended,
Kedron crossed, his journey ended;
And, as he nears her looming walls,
The gladdening sight his strength recalls.

But hark! What awful shrieks are those
That break the peaceful night's repose?
Two darksome forms, like goblins grim,
Weird antics cut in the starlight dim:

Advancing—retreating—a parry, a thrust,
Now having the 'vantage, now prone in the
    dust—
Ha! See! The traveler's gleaming knife
Has all but reached the bandit's life!
But the groan suppressed by an iron will
His mettle proves, though bandit still;
E'en wounded, yet he scowls disdain,
The gash ignores, unheeds the pain:
He scorns to cringe—but with a bound,
Hurls, crushed, his victim to the ground!

'Twas morn in ancient Palestine,
The air was hushed, the sky serene;
No leaflet stirred, no warbler sang;
Yet nature seemed to feel a pang.
But why? The dewdrop sparkled still,
Fair blossoms scented vale and hill,
E'en the sunward sky poured forth its flood,
Its red, inverted sea of blood.

Ho! Barabbas, ho! Hear Pilate's decree:
The Nazarene dieth, but thou goest free!
Off went the shackles, and forth from the cell
Stepped the bold felon; then followed the yell,
The cry of despair, and of anguish, and pain,
As the door of the dungeon swung to again.

Yet within the walls of that living grave
Was a bandit bad—but a bandit brave;
He was one of the three in that prison-room
Who hopelessly waited a terrible doom;
Yet he stood with his arms athwart his breast,
And the measured rise and fall of the chest,
With the sweeping glance of his fearless eye,
All told of a villain that dared to die!

Already there floated within the gate
Wild rumors of how they met their fate,—
Of the earnest though haughty mien of him
Who shuddered and writhed on an outer limb;
Of the One who imploringly raised his eyes,
Who seemed to be gazing beyond the skies;
Of another who jeered in the jaws of death,
And cursed the law with his waning breath;
Of the which should be first or latest to die,
As happened the thoughts of the passers-by.

But out on the road as ye move along,
Behold the returning, the sated throng!
Press onward and upward—thrust them aside;
Their flush of confusion shall be your guide;
Halt!   Rigidly, grimly, there hang the three—
On the veriest crest of Calvary!
Look at the sunken the bloodshot eye
Of the raving blasphemer about to die:

Note how he gasps, how he twists with pain,
Cursing, and cursing, yet cursing in vain!
And the one in the centre, say, who is He
Whom the soldiers and rabble press round to see?
What legend of crime, what sign of disgrace,
That flutters and flares at the populace?
Come read what is writ o'er the victim's head—
Soft! Ye must move with a reverent tread.

And thus run the words that your eyes peruse:
Jesus of Nazareth, the King of the Jews!
A bandit hath seen them and read them, too,
And he scans them again, like the thing were
    new;
And each time the meek Monarch breathes forth
    a prayer
It seemeth to lessen the robber's despair,
For the proud look of courage fades out from
    his face,
And a tender expression beams forth in its place.
Perhaps as the soul is about to take flight,
New scenes glad the view of its wondering sight,
As mariners nearing a newly-found shore
Gaze enraptured on beauties unheard of before.

Still he dwells on the face of the crucified King,
Nor gives heed to the shouts that derisively
    ring;

On the thorn-tortured brow, on the dry, moving
    lips,
On the blood that adown the pale cheek slowly
    drips;
All, all meet his gaze, and he utters a sigh,
While a single bright tear-drop starts forth from
    his eye.
As the pain-stricken babe to its mother reveals,
By the language of looks, the keen anguish it
    feels,
So the robber's sad glances now seem to impart
To yon Jesus the weight of remorse at his heart.

"Remember me, Lord!" Hear the bandit im-
    plore!
He whom life could not tempt to crave pity
    before.
What strange fascination hath conquered the
    thief?
What power converts to the mystic belief?
And the merciful Jesus replies from the tree:
"In Paradise with me this day shalt thou be!"

———

Oh, love is the victor that taketh the heart,
Than the lightning 'tis swifter, and stronger
    than art;
In the sea, in the earth, in the heavens above,
There dwelleth no power more mighty than love!

Easter Morn.

Cloudless the day was dawning,
  Yet silent the city slept,
And pure in the light of morning
  Gleamed the tears that the night had wept;
An odor like incense floated
  From many a petal rare,
And the boughs by the soft breeze smoted
  Made a rustle like wings in air.

Fan-like the beams, rose-tinted,
  Shot up from the eastern sky,
And the streamlet's waters glinted
  On that morn of victory.
The night of doubt was ended,
  And sweet on the morning's breath
Came the sound of voices blended,
  Singing of conquered death.

Glory to God, and glory
  Be Thine, triumphant King!
Let man repeat the story
  Till earth with pæens shall ring.
O Christ! as Thou ascended,
  All free from nail and thorn,
May we, from death defended,
  Each have our Easter Morn.

(125)

Nothing to Wear.

Toby Simpson, a dealer most worthy and just,
Slowly wended his way through the rattle and
    dust
Of the city.   He mused on the cholera scare,
On his relative chance as a wheat or a tare
In the prophesied raid. Then he mumbled a
    prayer,
And each mud hole he eyed seemed a villainous
    snare,
While his conscience said, solemnly, "Simpson,
    beware!"

On the strength of a limited balance in cash
He had planned for himself and his family a dash
To the mountains, the seaside, it mattered not
    where;
To delay any longer was more than he dare;
Some relief must be had from the terrible flare
Of the midsummer sun, which would surely impair
The good health of Dame Simpson, now cross as
    a bear.

'Twas quite late in July and old Sol was aglow,
All the people had gone who had money to go
From the city to seek a few sniffs of fresh air,
And forget for a season their burdens of care;

Then no wonder Dame Simpson was heard to
declare

That the Joneses looked up with an insolent
stare,

As she stood at her window exposed to the glare.

But her husband that ev'ning when rising from
tea,

With his hands full of tickets and heart full of
glee,

Quite as proud as a lion could be in its lair,

Shouted out: "To the Capes, yes, to-morrow,
prepare,

I've engaged jolly quarters and paid all the fare!"

To which mother and daughters, with mock
debonair,

Chorused forth: "Why, dear papa, we've nothing to wear!"

With a look most bewildered he clutched at a
tray,

For his mercantile courage was oozing away,

And his features were grim 'neath his carroty
hair;

Twenty bills he had paid for goods costly and
rare

For those females! and now could not possibly
spare

An additional dime.   Unaccustomed to swear,
It was startling to hear him say: "Darned if it's
    fair!"

In an eight by ten office, half sweltered with heat,
Sat T. Simpson, the jobber.   He gazed at his
    feet
Which reposed on a desk, just in front of his
    chair,
While his face was dejected and full of despair;
And he owed not a cent; his accounts were all
    square—
No, not that, but the problem of Nothing to Wear
Was just why the poor fellow sat pondering there.

Mortality.

You must die,
Spite of how you scheme or try;
Ghastly theme to contemplate!
Yet 'tis true beyond debate—
True that patient death will wait,
Silent wait and watch us keen,
Ever near, but never seen.
Be his wait though short or long,
When he grasps his grip is strong;
Useless shudder, bootless sigh,
> You must die;
> So must I.

All things die,
Though they leap or swim or fly;
Though they run or slowly crawl,
Microscopic, huge or small,
Death will strike them one and all.
Whence life comes or where it goes
Many guess, but no one knows;
Nature well her secret keeps;
Still the Greedy Monarch reaps.
If you ask me, I reply:
> All must die;
> So must I.

Fie, O fie!
Since you dare not this deny,
Why keep up the ceaseless fight,
Brooding, hoarding, day and night?
Why not by yourself do right?
Followed bliss is fleet of wing;
Caught, will disappointment bring.
Joy that seems so far away
Lies within your reach to-day.
Take it ere it passes by—
      Ere we die;
      You and I.

      Fame's a lie,
Left to mock us when we die;
Dead, then dead to shaft and plume.
Banquets spread upon the tomb
Will not light its lonely gloom.
Praise post-mortem (joke refined)
Flatters those we leave behind.
Place the laurels on the brow;
Give your gifts, your heart-love now,
Ere the golden chance slips by—
      Ere you die;
      As must I.

General U. S. Grant.

Go search the annals of the human race,
Go hear the legends that the heathen tell,
And learn that hist'ry, sacred or profane,
Records no hero like the mighty Grant.
Columbia proudly claims him as her own
And rears her monuments with love and pride;
But millions scattered o'er the face of earth,
And millions yet unborn, will share that claim:
Who serves mankind is deemed the friend of man,
And nations nationalize him in their hearts.
Since that first famous Battle of the Kings,
Of which we read in holy writ, no sword
E'er leaped from scabbard in a juster war
Than that which made our country free indeed,
Which, until then, was only free in name.
The bond of unity that Washington
To us bequeathed, Grant's loyal arm maintained;
Emancipation of the dusky race
By Lincoln's heaven-inspired pen, by Grant's
Unsullied sword was made complete!

                      How well
He proved the potency of equal rights,
And how he dignified Democracy
The monarchs of the world have told, thrice told,
In homage, hospitality and love.

No land is free where dwells a slave: to-day
In all our land there dwells no slave, and we
Are free, forever free!

     "Let us have peace."
Clasp hands across the ashes of the dead.
No, no; Grant is not dead, he cannot die;
The body is the worn-out coat of mail,
That with his sword and shield the warrior casts
Aside when life's campaign is o'er, and home,
Eternal home, is reached.

      He is not dead
Whose power still exists; and Grant will live
A life of immortality while yet
Our starry banner floats for liberty,
Which, thanks to God, will be forevermore.

Faith.

Beyond the darkest clouds
 The silent stars are gleaming;
And e'en though lost to sight,
 The sun is ever beaming:
Take heart, O soul, in sorrow,
 Though gloomy be thy way,
The Master-hand still guides thee
 As safe by night as day.

The Dying Child.

It is midnight. Hark! the old clock whirs:
  'Tis striking now the solemn tones
That mark the advent of another day.
  I've been dozing—sh!—my baby stirs—
Ah, how the little darling moans!
  There, pet, let mamma kiss the pain away.
      All alone! Thou God, in mercy
      Spare, oh, spare my precious child!

Weary watching: hours ne'er seemed so long.
  How dry and hot its throbbing brow,
How restless moves its tiny, pillowed head:
  What, awake, love! *Mamma sing a song?*
Why, yes, sweet child, I'll sing it now,
  So close your eyes and nestle in your bed.
      "Hush, my dear, lie still and slumber,
      Holy angels guard thy bed."

Day is breaking: far off gleams the dawn:
  Perhaps I now may steal some rest,
For baby sleeps as calmly as of old.
  I feel so strangely wretched and forlorn:
A weight seems bearing on my breast;
  I'll kiss my angel first, and then—how cold!
      Oh, my child, my poor dead baby!
      Father, let Thy will be done.

(133)

General Robert E. Lee.*

Let glory's wreath rest on the warrior's tomb,
Let monumental shaft surmount his grave,
For all the world yields homage to the brave,
And heroes dead have vanquished ev'ry foe.
The earth is strewn with storied slabs which tell
That manliness is born of every clime.
Each sword is drawn to guard a seeming right,
Each blow is struck to crush a fancied wrong;
For war proclaims sincere consistency,
And victory but seals just heaven's decree.
O Western World, what noble men are thine,
How brave their hearts, how steadfast to the end!
The pride of empire is of valor born,
The soldier shapes the destiny of man.
Look, then, ye tyrant kings that rule by fear!
Behold, ye nations of the earth! Our sons
Are warriors born: Lee was our son; he sleeps—
Our son, a soldier, an American.

---

* This poem was forwarded to the Lee Monument Association by
General Buckner, in the following letter :—

FRANKFORT, KY., May 15, 1890.

TO PRESIDENT LEE MONUMENT ASSOCIATION, RICHMOND, VA.

Dear Sir :—I enclose a communication from Mr. Geo. M. Vickers,
of Philadelphia, who was a soldier in the U. S. Army during the
Civil War, transmitting a poem written by himself in honor of the
memory of our greatest Southern leader. It was my purpose to

Minnie.

When the wild March winds were blowing,
　　When the snow lay drifted high,
First I heard your infant crowing,
　　First beheld your dark brown eye.

Storms have raged and snows have drifted,
　　Vanished, too, 'neath sunny skies
Many times since first I lifted,
　　Hugged and kissed our tiny prize.

Shield, O Lord, from harm our treasure,
　　Guide her with Thy holy love;
Mingle with each earthly pleasure
　　Joy that has its source above.

May she emulate her mother;
　　Meet with friends where'er she goes;
Know no storm in life—no other
　　Worse than March's winds and snows.

have handed this poem to you in person, if I had been able to be present on the occasion of the unveiling of the statue of General Lee.

　　As official engagements will probably preclude the possibility of my attendance, I do not feel at liberty longer to withhold from you a literary production which does honor alike to the memory of the great American soldier and to the patriotism of the writer of the poem. 　　　　　Respectfully, 　　　　S. B. BUCKNER.

Life's Battle.

St. John xvi. 33.

What life hath not sorrow,
  What soul but doth crave
A bliss for the morrow—
  Oft found in the grave?
Who feels his heart beating,
  Who heaves forth a sigh,
But knows that life's fleeting—
  Eternity's nigh?

Gay, thoughtless, or solemn,
  Humanity plods,
Till reacheth the column
  The City of Sods:
There brave ones shall wither
  No less than the shy;
All roads lead us thither,
  We journey to die.

Yet after the aching
  Comes soul-soothing peace;
When daylight is breaking,
  Then night-terrors cease.
Have faith in thy Maker,
  Look sometimes above—
Thou'lt then be partaker
  Of Hope and of Love.

(136)

Press on weary mortal
   And be of good cheer,
For at the bright portal
   Doth Jesus appear,
While hosts are attending
   To light thy dark way,
From danger defending
   Till dawneth the day.

Glory.

Already the tombs are crumbling,
   Already the weeds have grown,
And lost is the grave and level
   Of many a brave unknown.

Oh, glory's an empty promise,
   A myth and a gilded lie;
It lures but to death the living,
   And vanishes when they die.

The sleek and the well-fed coward
   That far from the battle keeps,
Gains more of the world's bright harvest
   Than bravery ever reaps.

The Moon.

Serenely, O moon, thou art beaming to-night,
Tracking the sea with thy silvery light;
Piercing the forest, thy beautiful rays
Are patching the ground in fantastical ways.

On city, on hamlet, on palace and hut,
On the far-stretching plain, in the deep mount-
    ain cut,
Thy mellow beams softly on all alike fall;
O queen of the night, thou hast homage from
    all:

From the glistening dew, from the true lover's
    sigh,
From the cricket's shrill voice and the katy-
    did's cry;
Thy heart-soft'ning power all races have felt;
To thy soothing appeal the most callous must
    melt.

O mute sympathizer, invoker of tales,
A fleet of heart secrets each night to thee sails.
To the shipwrecked at sea, when the storm
    clears away
And calm night succeeds the wild, boisterous day,

All huddled on raft, or faint clinging to spar,
There's a hope in thy beams that no danger can
    mar.

When red in the east thou ascendest the sky,
And thy disc meets the half-naked savage's eye,
He pauses, and feels as he views thy bright light
That a Greater than he is displaying His might.
Ere since by Omnipotence whirled into space,
Thou hast gladdened the night with thy radiant
    face.

To nations long dead, unrecorded by man,
Thou wast familiar when first they began,
Through their ages of splendor, their waning
    away,
Till their last mould'ring relic succumbed to
    decay.

And so, till Jehovah's dread voice bids thee stay,
And the night is absorbed by Eternity's day,
Thou shalt in thine orbit thy mission pursue,
A bright silver ship in an ocean of blue.

The Rusty Sword.

In a little roadside cottage, half hid by shrubs
    and vines,
A woman, old and feeble, on a faded couch
    reclines;
Her face is sweet, but sorrow has left its imprint
    there,
And her voice tells not the burden that her God
    hath bid her bear.

As I drink the limpid water from the homely,
    dripping gourd,
I note on the wall before me a naked, rusty
    sword.
I glance at the aged woman, and speaking she
    bows her head:
" 'Twas worn by a gallant soldier, for many a
    long year dead.

"One day, sir, I was looking where the road
    winds over there,
Wishing the war was over and breathing a
    mother's prayer—
I saw a wagon coming, and soldiers, all moving
    slow;
They were bringing my boy home, wounded—
    ah! it's many a year ago.

"I buried him there, by those willows—as you
    pass you can see his grave;
Oh, stranger, my child was a comfort, but his
    heart it was true and brave!"
Watching the pearls drop downward over her
    aged face,
I mount, and I ride in silence away from the
    lonely place.

But now I have reached the willows, and I leap
    to the shady ground;
I gather some wayside flowers to throw on his
    mossy mound.
I care not if Grant has led him, nor if he has
    fought with Lee;
I am an American soldier—and so was he.

Christmas Bells.

Ring on, ye bells of Christmas,
    Herald the joyous day!
Ring for the loved ones near us,
    For the wanderers, far away.

O Christmas bells, give courage
    To hearts that would do right;
Like the tender, Lowly Teacher,
    Tell us of love to-night!

The New Rosette.*

Let us sing a song
   That all may hear;
Sound the death of wrong,
   The knell of fear;
For in this cordial clasp of hands
America united stands:
     The new rosette
       Of Blue and Gray,
     Without regret,
       Is worn to-day.

Fire the signal gun,
   Proclaim our creed;
Liberty has won,
   And we are freed;
Our country's creed is Liberty,
And Freedom shall our watchword be;
     The new rosette
       Of Blue and Gray,
     Love's amulet,
       Shall be to-day.

* Rendered at the reunion of the Union and Confederate Veterans at Washington, September 16, 1896, by Miss Louise Nanette Orudorf, of Baltimore.

Ring the bells with pride,
 The brave are here;
Heroes true and tried,
 And each a peer;
Their deeds and valor e'er shall be
Our caveat on land and sea.
  The new rosette
   Of Blue and Gray,
  A pledge, a threat,
   Is worn to-day.

Give the armies praise,
 Of Grant, of Lee,
Shafts in honor raise,
 That all may see;
Proclaim that as they did, so we
Would do and die for Liberty;
  The new rosette
   Of Blue and Gray
  Bids none forget
   Their dead to-day.

Let the broadsides roar
 From ship to ship;
Shout your cheers from shore,
 Let colors dip;
Brave Farragut, Buchanan, too,
Showed what our gallant tars can do.

The new rosette
　　Of Blue and Gray,
Shall homage get
　　From all to-day.

Give thanks to God,
　That we are one;
He withholds the rod,
　Our strife is done;
One flag alone shall o'er us wave,
One Country, or for each a grave.
　　The new rosette
　　　Of Blue and Gray,
　　With love's tears wet,
　　　Is worn to-day.

Only a Pension Pauper.

"Look out!" Too late, the horses
   Trembling above him stood,
While the frightened, white-faced driver
   Was doing the best he could.

I stooped, and gently drew him
   From the mud where he groaning lay,
And I heard a man in the carriage
   To the waiting driver say:

" 'Tis only a pension pauper,
   Drive on, why tarry here?"
Then a crack of the whip made answer
   To the master's haughty sneer.

The carriage away was driven,
   But the injured man remained
On the sidewalk, pale and bleeding,
   With his clothes all torn and stained.

On his coat lapel was a button
   Of bronze, which no wealth can win,
And it told of a heart's devotion,
   Of war, and its awful din.

Yet the haughty man in his carriage
   But spoke as full many speak,
And forgot, ere he reached his office,
   Both the man and his piercing shriek.

But with all his bold defiance,
   He would rather have begged his food,
Than one instant have stood in battle
   Where for hours that "pauper" stood.

When I think of the early 'Sixties,
   Of the faces so fresh and fair,
Of the rosy cheeks so youthful
   Of the flowing, glossy hair;

When I see our sons and daughters
   That our comfort are to-day,
'Tis only the sight seen over
   Of an olden, bygone day.

And yet, if to-day 'twere needed,
   Our boys would be just as brave,
Though it cost them a life's ambition,
   Though they marched to a soldier's grave.

But neither the life's ambition,
   Nor death would be all they'd give,
The bitterest fate to many
   Would be to be spared to live—

To live when all life's best chances
Forever have passed away;
To live as "a pension pauper,"
Neglected, and old, and gray.

A Soldier's Offering.

The laurel wreath of glory
That decks the soldier's grave,
Is but the finished story,—
The record of the brave;
And he who dared the danger,
Who battled well and true,
To honor was no stranger,
Though garbed in gray or blue.

Go, strip your choicest bowers,
Where blossoms sweet abound,
Then scatter free your flowers
Upon each moss-grown mound.
Though shaded by the North's tall pine
Or South's palmetto tree,
Let sprays that soldiers' graves entwine,
A soldier's tribute be.

A Gentleman.

The appellation ''gentleman''
   Too frequently is bought,
But how *to be* a gentleman
   Is very seldom taught.

In vain the tailor's subtle skill,
   In vain the barber's art;
They cannot give one attribute,
   One polished grace impart.

A man may be a gentleman
   Though clad in homespun stuff,
And prove himself by word and deed
   A diamond in the rough.

No contact with the vulgar mind
   Can cloud his lustre o'er,
But like the lapidary's touch
   'Twill make him shine the more.

At home, abroad, to high, to low,
   He always is the same;
By this you'll know your gentleman
   Is worthy of the name.

The Old Canteen.

Of all the faithful friends we had
On weary march, when gay or sad;
Of all the comforts ever nigh
When throats were parched, when lips were dry,
Oh, comrades, none there was, I ween,
More welcome than
                    Our Old Canteen.

When powder grimed our faces black,
'Mid cannon's roar and rifle's crack;
When charging brave the foe to meet,
When falling back from grim defeat;
One thing we had on which to lean,
Our bosom friend,
                    The Old Canteen.

How oft the wounded's lips have pressed
The old tin spout whose water blest;
How oft when on the battle-field
The soldier's eyes in death were sealed,
A smile upon his face was seen—
Asleep, beside
                    His Old Canteen.

(149)

Ah, comrades, if there is one thing
Which memories from the past can bring,
One symbol that in time's swift flow
Binds hearts to friends of long ago,
'Tis this—enwreathed with laurels green—
The soldier's friend,
The Old Canteen.

True Love.

Since love is pure and holy,
    Unsought to mortals given;
Since God is love, and angels
    Are ruled by love in heaven;
How can true love be sinful,
    Or in false hearts abide,
When God Himself hath made it,
    When for its sake He died?

No, no, I'll not believe it!
    Life's sweetest joy is this—
This love, that all surpasses,
    This goal of human bliss:
The only cloud love brings us,
    Its only bitter pain,
That leaves the heart a desert,
    Is when we love in vain.

Twilight.

In solitude at twilight hour,
    Our natures softer grow.
And thought reverts, with wondrous power,
    To scenes of long ago.

The solemn whisp'ring of the wind
    Seems tuned to lull our care,
And plays—unto the dreamy mind—
    Some half-forgotten air.

Perhaps remorse may cause a sigh
    To 'scape the guilty breast,
As phantoms of the past flit by
    And mar its wonted rest.

But, oh, when early love appears,
    Just as we thought it then!
We press it to the heart it sears,
    As though it lived again.

'Tis then the lost "what might have been"
    Steals back to mock our fate,
And rouse the wish—which is but sin—
    When wishing comes too late.

(151)

O mystic hour! with visions fraught
Of forms and days gone by
Why these sad longings—all unsought—
Say, canst thou tell me why?

The Dear Old Sabbath.

Hold fast to the dear old Sabbath,
To the day of peaceful rest;
Look back to the days of childhood
That its tranquil glories blest;
Hold fast to its quiet pleasures,
All its sweet traditions save,
For the sake of the weary living,
And the memories of the grave.

Hold fast to the dear old Sabbath,
That is neared, like a verdant isle
On the week's dull sea of toiling,
With a thankful, happy smile.
One day give the Great Creator,
Be thy creed whate'er it may;
For the sake of human freedom
Keep the dear old Sabbath day.

Go Fan Yourself.

When moist with perspiration,
    When the mercury is high,
When stung to aggravation,
    When your tongue and lips are dry,
Then fretting's worse than folly,
    Rather let this be your rule—
Shake off all melancholy,
    Go and fan yourself—keep cool.

Go fan yourself, cease growling,
    Just remember who you are;
Stop snarling, snapping, scowling
    It will pay you better far.
If toiling melts your collars,
    Recollect that life's a school—
That all the lucky scholars
    Win the prize by keeping cool.

Go fan yourself when heated,
    Set the motto to a tune,
And let it be repeated
    Though December 'tis or June;
Since mortal man is fickle
    And his brother oft doth fool,
Just keep the saw in pickle,
    Go and fan yourself—keep cool.

(153)

The Palmetto and the Pine.

While the months to years are fleeting
　　Like a river's ceaseless flow,
And the landmarks old grow dimmer
　　In the distant long ago,
Let us glance once more behind us,
　　Where our battle days were seen,
Where our blood, like holly berries,
　　Sprinkled thick the grassy green.

There, in rifle pit, on ramparts,
　　Or upon the open field,
Come the visions of battalions
　　That would rather die than yield—
Come the stately forms of vessels
　　With their crews of sailors brave,
Whose memorial crests of glory
　　Are the white caps of the wave.

Once these men were happy, peaceful,
　　Till that bloody war, and then—
When it ended they turned homeward
　　From their dead to peace again.
Why they fought, who lost, who triumphed,
　　Who was wrong, or who was right,
Matters not; they were our brothers,
　　And were not afraid to fight.

'Neath the fairest flag that flutters
    Under heaven's azure dome
Dwell these warriors and their children
    In sweet Freedom's chosen home.
In his heart each holds a welcome
    For the soldier at his door,
And he never stops to question
    Which the uniform he wore.

We were soldiers, only soldiers
    Of the nation let us be.
Let us meet and greet as comrades
    Though we fought with Grant or Lee;
Let us form a noble order
    With sweet Freedom for our shrine,
And for each enwreathe a token—
    The Palmetto and the Pine.

Jehovah.

The splendor of Jehovah's work
    In ev'ry clime is seen,
Though at the barren, icy North,
    Or 'mid the Tropics green:

The Power that made what we adore,
    All beauteous things that be,
Hath power to wrought still grander scenes
    To greet our souls when free!

The Mother-in-Law.

While hearts are gay and tributes flow
In praise of those whose worth we know;
While hands are clasped and lips are pressed
And friendly welcome greets each guest,
Forget not that sweet womanhood
Whose love the test of years has stood,
Whose only wish is for our good—
                    The Mother-in-Law.

And so each mother, kind and true
Whose tender voice some child once knew,
Whose tired arms have oft caressed
The infant nestling on her breast,
May one day from her darling part;
Then two lives will entwine her heart,
Then she becomes just what thou art—
                    A Mother-in-Law.

A Kiss.

A kiss is the soul of eloquence,
    Love's sweet, though brief, refrain;
The true heart's golden recompense,
    In sorrow, peace or pain.

The New Year.

O welcome, welcome, bright New Year,
With joy we see thy dawn appear!
Farewell, Old Year of bliss and pain,
For never shall we meet again:
Go join the ages past and gone,
To-day we greet the New Year's morn.
Ring merrily each gladsome bell;
Let hearts with hope and pleasure swell;
Forget the words so harshly spoken,
Forgive the vows so coldly broken;
The Old Year's dead, the New is born;
Let smiles and love its birth adorn;
Begin the onward march anew
With earnest effort, brave and true;
To you, while time and life are fleeting,
May each year bring a joyous greeting:
Farewell the Old, all hail the New,
And a happy prosp'rous year to you!

February.

Under the drifts of virgin snow,
Many a bud is hiding low,
   Waiting the voice of spring;
Soon will the sap begin to flow
Bearing its fleet of leaves to blow;
   Soon will the blue-bird sing.

Whistle ye winds, while yet ye may,
Toss ye the barren boughs in play,
   Beautiful spring is nigh:
Speed thee, old winter, oh speed away!
Go with the skate and merry sleigh!
   Now must we say good-bye.

The Cynic.

Life is a mystery past finding out,
And faith in God has less of hope than doubt.
Men bow and say, Good Providence is right,
And try in gloom to find the sunbeam bright;
Yet since the day when thoughtful Adam fell
Has calmest reason taught us to rebel,
And mortal judgment of the chast'ning rod
Makes monstrous demon of the living God.
So would I bend to That which ruleth all,
Nor, like proud Satan, think, and fall.

(158)

Little Miss Lou.

Leisurely walking the meadows through,
Gathering daisies and violets blue
      Comes Little Miss Lou.
Empty her basket swings on her arm,
Free is her mind from a thought of harm,
And, somehow, her face has a power to charm,
      She seems so true,
      This Little Miss Lou.

But, sometimes (of course 'tis 'twixt me and you),
She looks very cute, even saucy, too,
      Does Little Miss Lou.
She clings to the daisies held in her hand,
As proud as a queen in a foreign land,
And her eyes say so plain that you'll understand,
      "Well, who are you?
      I'm Little Miss Lou!"

Far in the far away years to come,
Perhaps she may sit in her own wee home,
      A matronly Lou.
And maybe she'll then at supper preside,
Or call for the children that playful hide,
For ev'ry young girl may become a bride;
      There are lots that do,
      My Little Miss Lou.

Her basket is empty, 'tis light as air,
But soon 'twill be heavy and hard to bear;
      Poor Little Miss Lou.
Yet bravely she'll carry it safely back,
Over the self-same meadow track:
The strength she possesses, and has the knack;
      For 'tis nothing new
      To Little Miss Lou.

Thus may the young maiden her path pursue,
With never a sigh, nor a thing to rue,
      Dear Little Miss Lou.
Courage gives hope to the young and old,
And faith makes the weakest of hearts grow bold,
But virtue is better than gems or gold;
      'Twill carry you through,
      Sweet Little Miss Lou.

Aunt Polly Green.

At last the cottage was rented
   That vacant had stood so long,
And the silent gloom of its chambers
   Gave way to mirth and song.
Ever since the sheriff sold it,
   And poor Dobson moved away,
Not a soul had crossed the threshold
   Till the strangers came in May;
Then the mold on the steps of marble
   Was scoured and well rinsed off,
And the packed dead leaves of autumn
   Were thrown from the dry pump trough;
And the windows were washed and polished,
   And the paints and floors were scrubbed,
While the knobs and hearthstone brasses
   Were cleaned and brightly rubbed.

Now right across the turnpike
   Lived old Aunt Polly Green,
And through the window lattice
   The cottage could be seen.
There wasn't a bed or mattress,
   There wasn't a thing untied,
Not a box, a trunk, or a bundle,
   But what Aunt Polly spied.

Such high-toned, stylish neighbors
  The village had never known;
And the family had no children—
  The folks were all full-grown;
That is, there were two young ladies,
  The husband and his wife,
"And she," said old Aunt Polly,
  "Hain't seen a bit of life."

And so Aunt Polly watched them,
  Oft heard the husband say,
"Good-bye, my love," when leaving
  His wife but for the day;
And when he came at sunset
  She saw them eager run,
Striving the wife and daughters
  To be the favored one;
And as Aunt Polly, peeping,
  Beheld his warm embrace,
And noted well the love-light
  That lit the mother's face,
She shook her head and muttered,
  "Them two hain't long been wed,
A pity for his first wife,
  Who's sleepin' cold and dead.

"The poor thing died heart-broken,
  Neglected by that brute,

Who, soon as she was buried,
   Began his new love suit,
I know it," said old Aunt Polly,
   "I see the hull thing through;
How kin he so forget her,
   Who always loved him true?"
And tears of woman's pity
   Streamed down Aunt Polly's face,
As in her mind she pictured
   The dead wife's resting-place.
"To think," sobbed good Aunt Polly,
   "How the daughters, too, behave,
When their poor and sainted mother
   Fills a lone, forgotten grave."

One day when old Aunt Polly
   Sat knitting, almost asleep,
When the shadows under the woodbine
   Eastward began to creep,
A rosy-cheeked, brown-eyed maiden
   Walked up to the kitchen door,
Where never a soul from the cottage
   Had dared to walk before:
'Tis true that she walked on tip-toe,
   And cautiously peered around;
But she smiled and courtesied sweetly
   When the one she sought was found:

"I rapped on the front door knocker,
    And wondered where you could be,
So I hope you will pardon my boldness
    In walking around to see."

"Boldness," said Polly, rising,
    And fixing her glasses straight,
"Boldness ain't nothin' now-'days,
    To some, at any rate.
Sit down in that cheer and tell me
    Who 'twas that sent you here;
And tell me how long ago, Miss,
    You lost your mother dear."
The girl stood still, astonished,
    She knew not what to say,
She wished herself in the cottage
    That stood across the way.
"Now don't stand there a sulkin',
    Have a little Christian shame,
Even if she is a bold one
    That bears your father's name."

"Madam, or Miss," said the maiden,
    "There's surely a great mistake,
Or else I must be dreaming—"
    "No you hain't, you're wide awake;
I blame your bold stepmother
    For learnin' you this deceit;

Now answer me true the question
　　Which again I must repeat—
When did you lose your mother,
　　And of what did the poor child die,
And wasn't her pale face pinched like,
　　And didn't she often sigh?
Horrors! jist look at the heathen,
　　A laughin' right in my face,
When speakin' about her mother,
　　In her last lone restin' place.

" You say you was sent to invite me
　　To the cottage over the way,
That to-night's the celebration
　　Of your mother's marriage day,
That this is the silver weddin',
　　Of that young and frisky thing,
That for five and twenty summers
　　She's wore her plain gold ring?
Well, looks they are deceivin',
　　Why her hair's not one mite gray,
And her cheek is like a lily
　　Gathered for Easter Day.
An' will I come? Yes, dearie;
　　But let me your pardon crave,
For I've been like an old fool weepin',
　　A mournin' an empty grave."

Fidelity.

The purest, best gem in the crown of our youth,
That outshines all the rest, is the diamond Truth;
For Truth is Fidelity, ever the same,
Though winning approval, or bearing the blame.

Be faithful, be true, never think of the cost,
Lest the work of a life in a moment be lost;
Though years must be spent to gain honor and
      fame,
How quick the transition from glory to shame!

Be true to yourself and you're faithful to all;
If Truth's your foundation you never can fall,
For Truth lives forever, though buried from
      sight,
And will rise to defend you, untarnished and
      bright.

Have pride in the thought that you dare to be
      true,
Let Truth be your armor what path you pursue;
Though the dog is Fidelity's emblem, you can
Show the world that fidelity dwells in a man!

November.

The rosy-red apples are peeping through
   The clustering leaves of bright gold and green,
   And snowy-white frost on the grass is seen
Where yesterday glistened the pearly dew;
The wreaths of blue smoke that so gently rise
   Above the wee cottage that decks the moor,
   But tell that the warm, sunny days are o'er,
And bid us prepare for the wintry skies.

The flowers are gone, and the birds flit by,
   Fast journeying on to a warmer clime,
   While out from the leaves and the frosty rime
A beautiful fern spray is peeping shy;
The rows of ripe corn that in stacks appear,
   The tinkle of bells from the sheep at play;
   And throngs of young nutters, with shouts so
     gay,
Proclaim that November at last is here.

Lyric Poems.

(169)

LYRIC POEMS.

The King's Kiss.

A king rode forth one summer morn, his vast
    domain to see;
Through fields of wheat and fields of corn, rode
    on his majesty:
Quoth he, "A mighty king am I; whate'er I
    say must be,
For none there lives that dare deny a favor asked
    by me."

The king in search of rest and shade, dismounted
    in a dell,
Where, drawing water, stood a maid beside a
    mossy well;
With courtly bow the thirsty king, the proffered
    draught received,
And as he drank, a gallant thing his royal mind
    conceived.

"Fair girl," said he, "those lips of thine were
    surely made to kiss,
And fain I'd press them close to mine, refuse me
    not that bliss."

"No, no," the blushing lass replied, "no kiss
  you'll get from me,
For I'm a true and promised bride, to one who's
  far at sea."

"I am the King," the monarch said, "must I
  be disobeyed?"
The maiden slowly dropped her head, and trem-
  bled, sore afraid:
Then looking up with marble face, and wet but
  brave blue eye,
Said she, "Ere thus my troth debase, within the
  well I die!"

"Enough," the conquered sovereign cried, "this
  ring in honor wear,
For truly have I found a bride, as pure as she
  is fair."
The king rode off a wiser man than oft is monarch's lot,
And deemed that naught was sweeter than the
  kiss he never got.

Names Upon the Sand.

We sat beneath the drooping willows,
  Where we oft had sat before,
Gazing on the foamy billows
  As they dashed upon the shore;
Tender were the words we'd spoken,
  When I saw her tiny hand
Trace within a ring unbroken
  Both our names upon the sand.

The golden sun was slowly sinking,
  Twilight gathered o'er the sea,
Still we lingered, fondly thinking,
  Dreaming of the days to be—
Future joys in fancy reaping—
  Thus we spent the happy day;
But the tide came onward sweeping
  And our names were washed away.

Though years have passed, I wander lonely,
  List'ning to the ocean's roar,
Sighing for one sweet face only,
  Lost to me for evermore:
Once my poor heart fondly cherished
  Hopes again to press her hand,
But in vain; alas, they perished
  Like our names upon the sand.

(173)

The Helmsman.

When I look down at the binnacle light,
  Sing Mary, O my bonny queen,
Or cast my eyes on the gathering night,
  My face is sober then, I ween;
For then I think of Casco Bay,
Of fields and lanes long miles away,
And 'tis then your form and smiles appear
And the wheelman then forgets to steer;
Then mates and master quickly cry:
     O ho, there!
O ho, there, wheelman, mind your eye!

When billows leap 'neath the bellowing gale,
  Sing Mary, O my bonny queen,
And aloft all hands are short'ning sail,
  My mind beholds a fairer scene,
For, darling, then I think of you,
Forgot is ship, forgot is crew,
And the rain-drop seems your parting tear,
And the wheelman then forgets to steer;
Then mates and master quickly cry:
     O ho, there!
O ho, there, wheelman, mind your eye!

But when at anchor we happen to lay,
　Sing Mary, O my bonny queen;
When reached at last is the sheltering bay,
　The hills all blooming fresh and green,
Then quickly am I at your side,
O Mary, sweetheart, true and tried,
And the day, dear love, I hope is near,
When your sailor will no longer steer;
Then mates and master cannot cry:
　　　O ho, there!
　　　O ho, there, wheelman!
O ho, there, wheelman, mind your eye!

The Captain's Story.

'Tis years, little pet, since it happened,
  Long years, and full many a day;
And the story began on a morning
  When Kitty was raking the hay:
The meadows were sweet with the flowers' per-
      fume,
  And the birds sang their matins so gay;
Oh, 'twas then, at her side, some one lost his
      poor heart
  When Kitty was raking the hay!

Your eyes they are bright, little darling;
  Some day a gay bride you will be;
And your true heart and hand will be won, love,
  But never, ah, never by me!
For down in the meadows lie buried the hopes
  That were fair as a sweet summer day,
And they died with a kiss in a moment of bliss
  When Kitty was raking the hay.

There's little to tell of the story,
  It ends in the same olden way:
A mistake, and two lives ever parted,
  Two warm hearts forever astray!

(176)

Your round rosy cheeks and your dark rippling
    hair
But recall a dream long passed away;
Ah! there'll never again be such moments as
    then—
When Kitty was raking the hay.

Words Beyond Recall.

Oft words are spoken,
  Words we would forget,
Whose sad remembrance
  Only brings regret;
Oft hearts are wounded
  By the things we say;
Oft words we utter
  Steal life's hopes away.

Go, if forgiveness
  Still you may obtain,
Spare needless anguish,
  Spare bitter pain;
For, of all sorrows
  That our lives befall,
May this be spared you—
  Words beyond recall.

The Fisherman's Bride.

With a smile and a kiss we said good-bye
   At our little cottage door,
And the rising red sun lit up the sky
   And made gold the rocky shore:
Then I stood and I watched the snowy sail
   As it faded far away,
And I thought how he risked the reef and gale
   And for me toiled ev'ry day.

On that day came a stranger tall and grand
   Who it seems had lost his way;
And I gave him a drink with trembling hand,
   But a word I could not say.
Oh, he bow'd like a gallant knight of old
   As I pointed o'er the lea;
And the warm summer air grew damp and cold,
   And the sun shone dim to me.

'Twas at night, in the storm, all chill and wet,
   That my fisher came again,
And the hearth it glowed bright, his chair was
     set,
   And our meal swung on the crane—

But to save me from death I could not smile,
  Though with all my soul I tried—
And he gave me a kiss, all free from guile,
  Me, his vain and foolish bride.

Heigh-ho, me; how false, how fair the sea!
  But such thoughts I must put aside.
Heigh-ho me; at work I, too, should be!
  'Tis the lot of a fisher's bride.

The Maiden's Wish.

Once in years gone by we wandered
  'Mid the tall and waving rye,
And the bright young moon was beaming
  In the far off western sky.
Oh, how sweetly then you told me
  Foolish me, a wish to make,
And to keep the wish a secret,
  Lest the mystic spell would break!

Oh, how earnest o'er my shoulder,
  Trembling, glanced I to the right
Where the crescent in her beauty
  Shed a soft and silv'ry light!
How I thought the wish I whispered
  To your heart was known so well,
That I only smiled with pleasure
  When you told me not to tell!

Oft in dreams again I wander
  'Mid the tall and waving rye,
Where a bright young moon is beaming
  In the far off western sky;
But I waken lone and sadly,
  For 'tis then I think of you,
Of a wish my poor heart treasures
  But that never yet came true.

(180)

By the Old Cathedral.

I stood by the elms that gently swayed
   Near the old cathedral door;
     And the deep-toned knell
     Of the vesper bell
   To my soul a message bore:
  It seemed like a voice from the dying day,
  And soft as the slanting sunset ray,
That full on the gray stone portal played.
    Then a dreamy rapture o'er me stole,
    And I heard the organ's thunder roll
As the surf of a far-off sea.
    "Ave Maria!"
       And the bell rang;
       And the choir sang,
    "Ave Maria!"
And the Master drew near to me.

I knelt on the leaves all dead and sere,
   And I heard the wind's low sigh,
     And a rustling sound
     On the leafy ground,
   As of some one passing by:
  I reached for the hem of the garment fair,
  But only the gloaming mist was there.

The sun had gone down and night was near;
    'Twas a season of calm and holy bliss,
    And it came like a loving mother's kiss,
And it went like a sad farewell.
    "Ave Maria!"
        And the bell rang;
        And the choir sang,
    "Ave Maria!"
And I woke from the mystic spell.

Beautiful Trees of the Wayside.

Beautiful trees of the wayside,
  Blest are their ample boughs green,
Casting their kind, cooling shadows,
  Lending a charm to each scene;
Cherish them, guard them from danger,
  Think of the good they will do;
Each one of love is a token
    An emblem of hearts that are true.
        Beautiful trees! Beautiful trees!
        We their friends will be.

Let us plant trees by the wayside
  Gladly our part let us do;
Make fair the pathways for others
  While we life's journey pursue;
Each lend a hand that is helping;
  Here, 'neath the broad heavens free,
Let us bestow on our country
    The gift that a blessing may be.
        Beautiful trees! Beautiful trees!
        We their friends will be.

Under the green, waving branches,
  Deep in the woodland and grove,
Hark how the birds trill their praises,
  List to their sweet songs of love!

Beautiful trees of the forest,
   Trees of the garden and field,
Spare them from needless destruction,
   That each may its fair bounty yield.
      Beautiful trees! Beautiful trees!
      We their friends will be.

Plant well the seeds that they fail not,
   God will keep watch while we sleep;
Soon in their freshness they'll bring us
   Joy that all freely may reap:
Let us plant trees by the wayside,
   Plant them, with love, everywhere;
Ours is the pleasure to give them,
   That others their blessings may share.
      Beautiful trees! Beautiful trees!
      We their friends will be.

The Proudest Ships.

(From the opera, " The Lightkeeper's Daughter.")

The proudest ships that sail the sea,
   The rarest gems from foreign shore,
With wealth of gold, were naught to me,
   Could I behold her smile no more.
To me, she's sunshine, warm and bright,
   That gleams life's gloomy shadows through,
My own, my darling heart's delight,
   My little Mattie, loved and true.

Her pure white cheek with color glows,
   When tender words she whispers low,
And then, 'tis like a damask rose
   That rests upon a bed of snow.
The world has faces deemed as fair,
   And loving hearts from guile as free,
Still is she far beyond compare,
   The sweetest flower on earth, to me.

No Mother's Love.

(From the opera, "The Lightkeeper's Daughter.")

I never knew a mother's love,
   A tender mother's gentle care;
Yet oft I watch the stars above
   Because I know her home is there:
And could I see her angel face,
   A pleasure pure and sweet 'twould be,
And fair would seem earth's darkest place,
   If there her form I could but see.

Ah, those that have a mother dear,
   Should spare the word that brings a sigh,
Nor let neglect bring forth a tear,
   To dim the mild and loving eye.
The friends of youth, tho' warm and true,
   Will soon forget the early tie,
E'en th' olden friendship cares subdue,
   But mother's love can never die.

Adjust Yourself.

(From the opera, " The Lightkeeper's Daughter.")

Adjust yourself and spare the wrinkles,
    Keep the lustre of your eye;
Behold each star, how gay it twinkles,
    Tho' the darkest cloud be nigh.
Adjust yourself to things and places,
    To circumstances, times and faces.
Life is life, in every station,
    Poverty, an aggravation,
Riches, mere accumulation,
    Social status, but a name,
Riches, mere accumulation,
    Trouble comes to all the same.

Adjust yourself, and growl to-morrow,
    Keep the smile upon your lip;
One-half the ills of life we borrow,
    Brace yourself, and mind your grip.
Adjust yourself to tide and weather,
    The gale is stronger than the feather,
Foolish he, that fights his master,
    Wisdom oft defeats disaster,
Care will kill, than colic, faster,
    Surly glances seldom pay.
Care will kill, than colic, faster,
    Pleasant looks oft win the day.

(186)

The Deserter.

(From the opera, " The Lightkeeper's Daughter.")

Oh! the life of a sailor is jolly and free,
And there's many a sight to be seen on the sea,
Yet it's hardly the sort of a billet for me;
For with bacon my stomach could never agree,
Nor with biscuit, molasses, nor government tea,
Nor with swigging salt broth with a single split
    pea.
So I left the old "Creeper," determined to be
A full crew of my own, or be scorched with a "D."

Oh! I love foreign waters and towns to explore,
Or to lean on a gun with a twenty-inch bore,
Or to tell pretty maids of the dread battle's
    roar,
How we piled up the limbs, and swabbed up the
    gore.
But I never took kindly to pulling an oar,
Nor admired the wide-bottomed pants that we
    wore,
Nor the muffin-shaped hats, still I wisely for-
    bore
From indulging in comments, but paddled ashore.

(187)

Poor Ting Loo.

(From the opera, " The Lightkeeper's Daughter.")

In an Oriental city,
Where the tea-plant blooms the while,
   Strayed a maiden and her lover, brave Ting
      Loo,
Her young heart was filled with pity,
For Ting Loo, with ghastly smile,
   Was about to say a long and sad adieu.

He would sail across the ocean,
And upon a far-off shore,
   Make a fortune, then return and wed his bride;
It was no erratic notion,
Oft had others gone before,
   And his dark eyes flashed with love and manly
      pride.

But another had his eyes on
This poor, unhappy pair,
   'Twas her daddy, a most wicked mandarin,
He owned tons of fragrant Hyson
And Oolong and brands most rare.
   But, unlike his tea, this parent was not green.

He whipped out a long toad-sticker,
Gave a yell, and made a spring,
   Full intending that Ting Loo should breathe
      no more,
But the young man being quicker,
Like a swallow on the wing,
   Flew, and let the aged pagan have the floor.

He took refuge in the water,
And our good ship passing by,
   Soon we fished him out and rigged him up in
      blue;
And the old man and his daughter
Watched us go with wistful eye,
   And to Yankee-land we sailed with poor Ting
      Loo.

The Maid from Londonderry.

(From the opera, " The Lightkeeper's Daughter.")

Och, I'm a maid from Londonderry,
Sure that's the place the folks are merry,
    Wid a twiddle de dee, an' a twiddle de da,
    Sure that is the spot where the folks are gay.
The ould piper he plays on her Majesty's green,
First a song for the shamrock, then one for the
        queen,
    An' if ever ye happen to go that way,
    Wid a twiddle de dee, an' a twiddle de da,
    Ye'll find that the folks there are mighty gay.

Och, I'm a maid from Londonderry,
Sure it's the place the folks are merry,
    Wid a twiddle de dee, an' a twiddle de da,
    Bad luck to the time when I came away.
Than ould Ireland no fairer land ever was
        seen,
Wid her fields an' her hills an' her valleys so
        green;
    An' there's little more now that I mane to
        say,
    Wid a twiddle de dee, an' a twiddle de da,
    An' that's that we'll thravel jist on our way,
    Wid a twiddle de dee, an' a twiddle de da.

Mermaids' Chorus.

(From the opera, " The Lightkeeper's Daughter.")

Oh, come to our home in the beautiful deep,
Where vines of bright green o'er the red coral
creep,
Fair mortal, come join us, and learn to forget
The cold world that gives thee but pain and
regret.
Come, come to our grotto and share the sweet
spell,
Come, rest on our couches of moss-covered
shell!
Oh, come to our home in the beautiful deep,
And gently the waters shall rock thee to sleep.

Oh, come to our home in the far away sea,
Where pleasures ne'er dreamed of are waiting
for thee!
Why heed not when fond voices call thee away?
Why linger when sorrow alone bids thee stay?
Then listen, fair maid, to our mystical vow:
A crown of bright gems shall encircle thy
brow!
Come, come! and with sceptre, our queen thou
shalt be;
Oh, come to our home in the beautiful sea.

The Lawyer's Song.

(From the opera, "The Lightkeeper's Daughter.")

Now this is a very singular case,
   And its magnitude I feel;
For I conquer a rogue both tricky and base,
   By a turn of fortune's wheel.
But, really, none but a lawyer can know
   How the shifting straws incline,
As the tenth point oft wins the case for the foe,
   Though possession gives us nine.

This merchant and maid will surely agree,
   That I've served them well and true;
For there's few in the law that could useful be
   On so small a revenue.
Ah! the law is a wonderful, queer sort of thing,
   And its sword is sharp and bright,
And a man to the breeze can with safety fling
   All his fear, if his cause be right.

But exceptions, tho' rare, I am told do occur,
   'Tis the fault of our modern school;
And the record must have an occasional blur,
   In proof of the golden rule.

Why, Why, O Sea?

Why, why, O sea, do the weary at heart
   Their burden of care to thy bosom confide?
Why in our bliss do we fondly impart
   All, all our joy to the cold, gleaming tide?
Sun, moon, nor stars kiss thy bosom in vain,
   For gladly they give back each ray in glee,
Tho' naught to me hast thou given but pain,
   Or poor, foolish dreams, yet I love thee, O sea!

Why, why, O heart, doth it lull thee to hear
   The song that forever the breakers have sung;
Ah, why, when each wave brings a message of
     fear
   And the waters are brine with the tears they
     have wrung?
Still, still the same do thy beauties beguile,
   And still from thy anger the bravest would flee,
Yet on thy coldness and dangers I smile,
   For with all thy false wooing, I love thee, O sea!

Whate'er My Fate.

(From the opera, " The Lightkeeper's Daughter.")

Whate'er my fate may be,
  One thought will help me bear it,
'Tis that I'm fondly loved by thee,
  That thou would'st gladly share it.
And should I perish, sad and lonely,
  One thought would make me sigh,
'Twould be the fond wish only,
  That we could say "good-bye."

Ah! why this sad regret,
  When all life's scenes are fleeting?
When faith and hope to me as yet
  Have proved but vain and cheating.
Still naught shall make me faint nor falter,
  No tear shall dim my eye,
No power can make me alter,
  Good-bye, my own, good-bye!

Only a Word at Parting.

I would not ask why you leave me,
  My fate too well I know;
I only ask you to give me
  One word before you go.
Only a word at parting,
  Only a last good-bye,
Only a word to spare you
  Many a weary sigh.
Go and forget that e'er we met;
  Go, like a bird, be free,
Light-hearted, gay, banish regret,
  Give not a thought for me.

The words that oft you have spoken
  Let faithless love unsay;
I only ask for one token,
  Before you go away.
Only a word at parting,
  Only a last good-bye,
Only a word to brighten
  Many a gloomy sky.
Summer may bring its birds to sing;
  Sweet may their gay songs flow;
Yet must they soon be on the wing,
  Pleasures but come to go.

(195)

Sweet buds that bloom fragrant to-day,
Soon like a dream wither away.
Only a word at parting,
Then let the false love die;
Tho' you may coldly leave me,
Give me a last good-bye.

The Coast Guard.

(From the opera, "The Lightkeeper's Daughter.")

When the tempest blows,
And the surf runs high,
When it hails or snows,
From a wild, weird sky;
'Tis then that we watch
Through the long, dark night,
For the minute gun,
Or the signal light
Of a vessel in distress.

When the awful cries
Of despair are heard,
When each foam-flake flies
Like a frightened bird,
Then quickly all
To the life-boat spring,
Or the doubtful line
From the mortar fling
To the vessel in distress.

Cloud Forms.

I sat alone on a summer day
   And watched the clouds on high,
As soft, and fleecy and white they lay
   Like mountains in the sky;
And as I gazed, in a sort of dream,
   And thought of years to be,
I saw a cot 'mid a rosy gleam
   That lit the cloudland lea:
The picture grew, and I saw a face
   As fresh, as sweet as May,
Then shadows came and I lost its trace,
   And the vision passed away.

That summer day has long passed away,
   The autumn chill is here;
The school bell rings and the children gay
   Heed not the dead leaves sere;
And near a cot stands a maiden fair
   With face as sweet as May,
And as I gaze on her beauty rare
   I think of a summer day—
A day when I watched the clouds on high
   And dreamed of years to be;
But cold and heedless she passes by,
   And her form no more I see.

I know not why I should give a sigh
  For one sweet passing face,
I only know that howe'er I try
  My heart still gives it place;
I only know that the world to me
  Is barren, lone and cold,
That life is drear and the things I see
  Seem dim, and worn and old:
Yet still I long and watch and wait,
  And shall until I die,
I wait to meet, though 'tis e'er so late,
  My vision of the sky.

Love's but a Dream.

Love's but a dream, a happy dream,
　　Whose pleasure brings but pain,
Love gives the heart of hope a gleam
　　To prove that hope is vain;
Yet love is life, it lights the way
　　Though black the stormy sky;
'Tis love that bids the spirit stay
　　That fain would homeward fly.

Love's but a dream, yet where's the heart
　　That, dreaming, would awake?
Dream on, for when love's dreams depart
　　Too oft the heart must break.
The path we tread, yet other feet,
　　Though weary, must pursue;
And pilgrim lips will e'er repeat
　　What love's sweet dream can do.

Then give me love, oh, let me love,
　　Though pain it brings or care;
If love's a dream, oh, let me move
　　Some breast that dream to share!

Fire Phantoms.

Now the coals are brightly glowing
  In the dear old-fashioned grate,
Cheerful rays about me throwing,
  And the hour is growing late;
Yet alone I sit and ponder
  Heedless of the stormy blast,
Till in fancy back I wander
  'Mid the scenes that long have past.

One by one forgotten pleasures
  To my dreamy gaze appear,
'Till a form my mem'ry treasures
  To my side seems drawing near:
'Tis a maiden proud and queenly,
  But as false as she is fair,
And her face that beams serenely
  Lured me almost to despair.

Now the embers fast are dying,
  And the light is growing less,
While the gale without is sighing
  Like a spirit in distress.
Oh, how oft I've read in flashes
  From the glow a fairer fate,
Yet my hopes have turned to ashes
  Like the embers in the grate.

The Rival Swains.

Tom and I were at the party,
  Tho' we only came by chance,
But our welcome being hearty,
  Both enjoyed the merry dance.
But ere long we each discovered
  That a damsel sweet and fair,
Near whose home we both oft hovered,
  Like ourselves had happen'd there.

Tom and I were all attention
  To the slightest word she said,
And we both took care to mention
  That the time had quickly fled,
For each hoped to have the pleasure
  Of escorting Lizzie home,
And my rapture knew no measure,
  When the time to go had come.

All our thoughts were then of marriage,
  As we both stood mutely there,
Tom with stylish horse and carriage,
  I with only Shanks' old mare,
When to break the spell I faltered—
  "Lizzie, will you walk or ride?"
Then I saw that things had altered,
  And that Tom had won a bride.

Oh, 'tis sweet to love a maiden,
   When she loves you for yourself,
But with sorrow you'll be laden,
   If she only loves your pelf.
Still I'm single, rather lonely,
   And would like a bonny bride,
So, now girls, I'll ask this only,
   "Who would rather walk than ride?"

Pretty Holly Berries.

Pretty holly berries,
   Oh, how bright you glow,
'Mid the green leaves nestling,
   Peeping through the snow;
Pretty holly berries,
   Though the boughs are bare,
You alone, to cheer us,
   Still your crimson wear.

Pretty holly berries,
   If we could but know
Why you love the winter,
   Why you love the snow;
If we could but guess it,
   If we on it fell,
Pretty holly berries,
   You would never tell.

God Bless Our Land.

Father, to Thee,
God of the free,
Trusting Thy mercy,
Thy children come;
Guide us aright,
Shield by Thy might,
Safe from all danger,
Sweet freedom's home.
Still may we welcome
Man oppressed,
Here may the weary
Find their rest;
Loyal to country
Firm let us stand,
Ever united,
God bless our land.

May love and peace,
That will not cease,
Bind us together
From strand to strand;
On shore or sea
Our song shall be,
God and our loved ones,
Home and our land.

(203)

God, our Creator,
Freedom's Friend,
From ev'ry danger
Us defend;
May we still prosper
Led by Thy hand;
Bless all our leaders,
God bless our land.

The Stars and Stripes Forever.

One flag alone shall wave above us,
　'Tis the emblem of the free,
And all the world shall pay it homage,
　Though it floats o'er land or sea.
Dear flag, with all our hearts we love thee,
　But thy foes we still defy!
Thou alone shall be the banner
　That our hands will raise on high.

One flag, one starry constellation
　In its ample field of blue;
One flag, whose folds shall ever bind us
　Firm together, keep us true;
In peace or war we will defend thee,
　Still our emblem thou shall be;
One flag alone shall wave above us,
　'Tis the banner of the free.

Donald Gray.

Poor Donald Gray, once happy and gay;
My heart it said yes, but my lips they said nay!
  Years on their journey are fleeting,
  Fond hearts that we loved have ceased beating,
  Still I'm silently, vainly entreating
For one word from my dear Donald Gray.
  Oh, could I recall what was spoken,
And recline on your bosom to-day,
  This spirit, now weary and broken,
    Forever would willingly say,
    Ah, yes, Donald Gray,
    From my soul, Donald Gray!

Poor, foolish me, once joyous and free,
Mistaken for life in a moment of glee!
  Oft when the day-beams are dying,
  When sadly the wild birds are crying,
  And the billows are mournfully sighing,
All alone do I watch by the sea.
  Oh, why is love's faith unavailing,
Do I hope for what never can be?
  Of all the proud ships that are sailing
    Not one brings a message to me;
    Yet all I can do
    Is to wait—wait—and see.

(205)

The Old Organ Blower.

I've pumped the bellows here for years,
I've heard devotion's hopes and fears;
I've watched the children in their bloom,
I've seen the bride, the happy groom;
And one by one I've seen them go;
I've heard the heartfelt sobs of woe;
The pastor, people, all I've seen
While pumping here behind the screen,
For though all things I plainly see
There's few indeed that gaze on me;
I pump, pump, pump,
And blow, blow, blow:
High in the organ loft I stand
And work the bar with trembling hand,
And blow, blow, blow!

When first I came in years gone by,
With raven locks and flashing eye,
The organ seemed to louder swell,
And softer, sweeter tales to tell;
But now my locks are silver gray,
The organ seems to sadly say,
The time grows near when I must go,
When I no longer here may blow.

(206)

The stained glass windows still subdue
The sunbeams warm that glimmer through;
The voices blend in solemn praise
As in the olden bygone days;
But those I loved no more appear,
No more they fill my heart with cheer;
Yet while I've strength on earth below,
Still in the organ loft I'll blow.

The Anchor Watch.

The gale is driving the foamy waves
  In their rush to the rock-bound shore,
The good ship's crew ev'ry danger braves
  And laughs at the breakers' roar;
For a faithful watch at the bow is set,
  The anchor and chain are strong,
And though cold, and oft with the sea spray wet,
  He sings of his love a song.

The bright sun gleams on the dancing sea,
  The morning is warm and fair;
And a maiden looks out from a cot in glee
  With never a thought of care;
But a spar and a rudder have come ashore,
  And a story they mutely tell,
Of a sailor who'll hie to his love no more,
  Of a maid, and her last farewell.

I'm Getting Too Big to Kiss.

The friends of my childhood with pleasure I greet,
  Their faces I ever hold dear,
In palace or cottage, on meadow or street,
  Wherever they chance to appear.
Then do not misjudge me, and deem me not cold,
  Nor call me a queer, haughty miss,
Oh, no one can budge me, so do not be bold,
  I'm getting too—too big to kiss.

'Tis hardly a year since the guests of the house,
  On leaving, would kiss me adieu,
The parson, the deacon, old Schnider Von Krouse,
  Ned Blanc, and the young squire, too.
They called me a treasure, a sweet, roguish maid;
  Now nonsense like that is amiss,
Though once 'twas a pleasure, I'm really afraid
  That somebody's too big to kiss.

Now if you should happen by moonlight to walk,
  With some one you know very well,
Remember 'tis harmless to laugh and to talk,
  Or sweet little stories to tell.
But oh, have a care, girls, and heed me, I pray,
  For what I would counsel is this—
Refuse, though his hair curls, and promptly this
    say:
  I'm getting, sir, too big to kiss.

Oh, no, no, no, no, sir! Allow me to pass;
  Oh, no, sir, 'tis more than I dare:
That game's out of fashion (I'm sorry, alas!)
  You needn't look cross as a bear.
Yet still I've an ember of pity right here,
  I'll throw you just one kiss like this,
But, sir, you'll remember, now don't come so
    near—
  That really I'm too big to kiss.

Because I Love You.

'Tis but a rose, a faded spray,
  That withered lies before me;
And mem'ries of a bygone day
  Are sadly stealing o'er me.
Tho' false you've been, I keep it still,
  But, oh, not to reprove you;
Its leaves I guard, and ever will,
  Dear one, because I love you.

'Tis but a song, a sweet refrain,
  That once you loved to sing me;
Yet rose and song are fraught with pain,
  And only sorrow bring me.
Tho' lost to me, tho' far away,
  My heart can ne'er reprove you,
The song I sing, I keep the spray,
  Dear one, because I love you!

14

Baby Bye.

Baby bye, hush-a-bye,
  Close your pretty, sleepy eyes;
Baby bye, sweetly lie,
  Angels watch you from the skies;
Soft is now your downy pillow,
  Free your tiny heart from care:
And so may it be
When life's mystic sea
  Baby's drifting bark shall bear.

Baby bye, hush-a-bye,
  Could you tell your dreams to me,
Baby bye, then would I
  Know the wonders that you see:
Go to sleep, my precious darling,
  Gathers fast the twilight gray;
Go to sleep and rest
In your peaceful nest—
  Rest, my baby, while you may!

Columbia, My Country.*

Columbia, my Country!
  My song is of thee,
Thy honor and glory
  Mine ever shall be;
From hillside, from valley,
  O'er mountain and plain,
Shall echo forever,
  Sweet freedom's refrain.

Columbia, my Country,
  Thou beautiful land!
The world in thy light shall be free!
May God keep me steadfast,
  In heart and in hand,
Still faithful, my Country, to thee!

Columbia, my Country!
  My heart thrills with love;
To thee am I loyal,
  God hears me above;
Thy foes are my foemen,
  To thee would I give
E'en life, were it needed,
  That freedom might live.

*The copyright was transferred to the United States Government
in 1893, giving all persons the right to publish the anthem.

Columbia, my Country!
    Earth's fairest domain,
I honor thy heroes
    Who for thee were slain;
Thy flag still the emblem
    Of freedom shall be,
Columbia, I love thee,
    Sweet home of the free.

The American's Farewell.

Farewell, farewell, my own dear land,
    This heart will ne'er deceive thee,
And as I watch thy fading strand
    I sigh because I leave thee;
The home I prize, the tearful eyes,
    The ties I leave behind me,
Though years I roam 'neath foreign skies,
    To thee in love shall bind me.

Farewell, farewell, each faithful heart,
    What joy whene'er I met thee;
And, oh, what pain it is to part,
    Yet I shall ne'er forget thee!
America, how sweet thy name;
    Still true thou'lt ever find me;
O land aglow with freedom's flame,
    To thee my love shall bind me.

Can Love Forget?

Oh, mother, do not ask me why
   My cheek has lost its bloom,
Nor why the brightness of my eye
   Is shadowed o'er with gloom:
The love I love has left for me
   But sighs and vain regret,
And this my song shall ever be—
   Alas, can love forget?

The leaves that fall and yellow grow
   Beneath the summer sky,
But mutely tell a tale of woe
   As zephyrs waft them by;
No, mother, do not ask, I pray,
   Why oft my eyes are wet;
For I alone would sing to-day
   My song—can love forget?

I'll gather me a fair bouquet
   Of pansies wet with dew,
And they to my false love shall say,
   That I at least am true;
Oh, love, 'twere better far for me
   That we had never met,
Since we must ever parted be—
   And yet can love forget?

The Old Ship.

'Tis years ago, my mates, that we,
   A happy, hardy crew,
Left port one summer day for sea,
   When that old ship was new.
Her spars were light and taper, too,
   Her sails were white as snow;
Then o'er the foam like a gull she flew,
   Yet that was long ago.

On that old ship hard fights were fought
   By sailors brave and true,
Whose sweethearts lived in ev'ry port
   From Bangor to Peru;
But oft Jack tars come back no more
   To sweetheart or to bride,
For some find homes on a far off shore,
   And some beneath the tide.

The grass on yonder shore is green,
   The tide drifts gently by,
But in the air there's something keen
   That dims your weather eye;
For mem'ry spreads each snowy sail,
   And crowds again the shore,
Where fair ones cheered, though their cheeks
     grew pale,
   All in the days of yore.

Yes, mates, we tell you true,
As many a lass and lad could tell
Who on her decks have said farewell
When that old ship was new.

The Ivy-Clad Ruin.

'Tis the old, old church that for years I've known,
And with ivy green are its walls o'ergrown;
All its ancient splendor has passed away,
And there's naught remaining but grim decay;
The pale moonbeams glimmer the windows
    through,
And the roofless floor is all damp with dew;
Both the pious priest and his flock are gone,
And the gravestones watch o'er their dead alone.

Oh, how oft I've passed thro' the spacious aisle
And have met the throng with a friendly smile;
In the bygone days when I saw them kneel,
When I felt the thrill of the organ's peal;
But the forms I knew enter here no more,
And no footsteps fall on the mouldy floor;
There's but one thing left that with life I've
    seen—
'Tis the faithful vine of the ivy green.

Song of the Chase.

Over the meadows we gayly sweep,
Over the ditches and rails we leap;
Huntsmen so gallant and ladies fair,
Proudly the panting chargers bear.
    Crack! crack! on we go;
    Loud, long the bugle blow!

Now in the valley, now out again,
Now 'mid the reapers of golden grain;
Eyes flashing brightly, cheeks aglow,
Merrily on to the chase we go.
    Crack! crack! ply the lash;
    On, on, still on we dash!

Swiftly before us the wild stag flies,
Bounding away from the hounds' fierce cries;
Up from the stubble the pheasant springs,
Shaking the dew from his gorgeous wings.
    Crack! crack! speed away;
    Quick! quick! the stag's at bay!

Hark to the sound that we love so well,
    Tally ho! Tally ho!
Hark to the echoes from cliff and dell,
    Tally ho! Tally ho!

Em'ly's Wedding.

We had played for years together,
  She had been my little bride,
And in childish love had promised
  Ne'er in life to leave my side;
But the seasons came and vanished,
  And my Em'ly older grew,
And my heart it held a secret
  That my playmate never knew.

One day as friends we parted,
  With a kiss we said "good bye;"
I was off to seek my fortune,
  Yet I never told her why:
But the story is an old one,
  It has oft been told before;
And while hearts must go unmated
  'Twill be told forevermore.

Once again, unseen, I saw her
  Leaning on another's arm,
And the organ's strain of triumph
  Seemed to bear a wondrous charm;
But to me, who stood a stranger,
  Each note seemed to bid me hide,
Lest my face should mar the pleasure
  Of the fair and happy bride.

Sweetheart Em'ly, happy, smiling,
  May her life from care be free,
May she ever know the pleasure
  That for me can never be;
Sweetheart Em'ly, how I loved her,
  She was light and life to me,
And I'll ever hide the sorrow
  That her true eyes must not see.

The Afterglow.

The sun will shine no more to-day,
  The gloaming fades, and night is near;
The clouds low down are ashen gray,
  Cold, bleak and gray; the night is here:
But high above the evening star,
  Like daylight loth to go,
With rosy blush, so faint, so far,
  Still gleams the afterglow.

Ah, me! it seems but yesterday,
  The love-lit bliss of olden years;
Ah, yes! the life dream melts away,
  Fades out 'mid smiles, oft dimmed by tears:
Yet in each heart there lingers still
  Some joy it used to know,
Which mem'ry brings with happy thrill
  To be our afterglow.

Unmated.

There is a life—I know not where—
  There is a true heart beating;
A breast my ev'ry sigh to share,
  Fond lips each prayer repeating;
    We may not meet this side the grave,
    And years o'er one the grass may wave;
But when, in realms of endless day,
  Are gone the bonds that bind me,
When earth's dark clouds have passed away,
  Dear one, I then shall find thee.

'Mid pleasure's charm I sigh regret,
  Because thou canst not share it;
Yet sorrow's gloom I'd soon forget,
  Couldst thou but help me bear it.
    The way is hard and friends are few,
    God only knows the false, the true.
But when the clouds have passed away,
  When gone the chains that bind me,
I know, in realms of endless day,
  My own, I then shall find thee.

Out on the Hills.

Out on the hills in silence,
  Out 'neath the starry sky,
Watching their flocks sat the shepherds,
  Watching and wondering why,
Wondering why the sweet music
  Came from the blue above;
Wond'ring at angel legions
  Singing a song of love.

Oh, 'twas a song of victory,
  A song of redemption too;
It told that a Mighty Prince was born,
  My soul, 'twas a song for you!

Out from the depths above them
  Shone a refulgent light,
Piercing the night's sombre shadows,
  Greeting the shepherds' glad sight;
Hark! 'tis the voice of an angel,
  Peace and goodwill to men,
Heavenward the hosts are soaring,
  Singing their song again.

Glory to God the Father,
  Glory to Christ, His Son,
Glory and praise to the Spirit,
  Glorious Trio in One;

Praise to the merciful Jesus,
    Honor Him ev'ry tongue,
Sing to His lasting glory,
    Sing as the angels sung.

Guard the Flag.*

Guard the flag, guard the flag of our native land,
    Guard the flag of liberty;
Guard well the flag with heart and hand,
    God save the banner of the free!
Sons of the nation, hold it aloft,
    Bravely its foes defy;
Our beautiful flag, the hope of the world,
    Ever shall wave on high!

Guard the flag, guard the flag that our fathers
      bore,
    Let its pride our glory be;
Oh, let it wave o'er sea and shore,
    The starry emblem of the free!
Though 'neath it marching onward to war,
    Though 'neath its folds in peace,
Our motto shall be to still guard the flag,
    Never our vigil cease.

*"Guard the Flag," is sung in Public Schools throughout the United States, and by Americans upon all patriotic occasions. It is now acknowledged to be one of our National Songs.

Blacksmith Joe.

In the town of Winkumtural,
  Many long, long years ago,
Lived a man who shod the horses,
  Whom the folks called Blacksmith Joe.
    Ah, 'tis a story that is full of woe;
        Poor Joe!
Oh, his face was always beaming
  In the merry, ruddy forge's glow,
Till a maiden brought a donkey
  To be shod by Blacksmith Joe.

Now this maiden was a beauty,
  Which, of course, right well she knew,
And poor Joseph gazed with rapture
  On her eyes of tender blue.
    Ah, rest assured that ev'ry word is true,
        Too true!
Said the blushing maiden sweetly,
  "Sir, I've many, many miles to go,
Will you kindly shoe my donkey?"
  "That will I," quoth Blacksmith Joe.

Soon his brown hand on the bellows
  Made the bright sparks upward fly,
While each silent watched the embers,
  With a far off, wistful eye.
    Ah, and they uttered such a doleful sigh—
        Oh, my!

(222)

All at once the wicked donkey
 With his naughty little foot let go,
And the maiden fell, unconscious,
 In the arms of Blacksmith Joe.

'Neath the elms they laid the maiden,
 Where the pansies love to grow,
And the forge was soon deserted
 By the broken-hearted Joe.
  Ah, and at last his trouble laid him low;
    Poor Joe!
When the pale young moon is shining,
 If you happen by the forge to go,
You will see a ghostly donkey,
 And the maiden's form with Joe.

Cling! clang! cling! clang!
Merrily rang his anvil,
  Many's the year ago;
Cling! clang! cling! clang!
Till the maid with her donkey
  Ended the peace of Joe.

Watching the Tide Drift By.

We stood by the stream, Nanette and I;
  Never a fear had we;
The silvery moon shone in the sky
  Glinting the dewy lea.
"Love that is true dies never"—
  This was her sweet reply,
When first we stood by the river
  Watching the tide drift by.

We stood by the stream, Nanette and I;
  Never a word said we;
The silvery moon shone in the sky
  Glinting the dewy lea.
Oh, that fond hearts should sever,
  Oh, that fair hopes should die!
Sadly we stood by the river
  Watching the tide drift by.

We stood by the stream, Nanette and I;
  Many's the day since then,
And many's the lip that said good bye,
  Never to meet again:
E'en though it be forever,
  Yet still our hearts reply,
As when we stood by the river
  Watching the tide drift by.

The Proud Flag of Freedom.

The proud flag of freedom, unsullied, behold
  How cluster about it the glories of years,
As skyward and westward, 'mid purple and gold,
  In the land of the sunset, its home, it appears.
America's token of faith never broken,
    Sweet signal that flutters o'er mountain and
      sea;
That mutely repeats what our fathers have
    spoken,
    That tells the oppressed they may come and be
      free!

O proud flag of freedom, how swells with delight
  The breast of the wand'rer who meets thee afar;
What home-visions come with the gladdening
    sight,
    And how fond dwells his eye on each stripe
      and each star!
Thus be it forever, while oceans may sever,
  Or fate hold in exile, a man from our shore!
Tho' fairer the clime, an American never
  Forgets his own colors, but loves them the more.

Thou proud flag of freedom, so lovely in peace,
  So awfully grand in the dread crash of war,
Float on in thy beauty till nations shall cease,
    While there's room in the blue for another
      bright star:

From danger defending, still onward, ascending;
   The hope of mankind and the envy of none:
"E Pluribus Unum," our motto transcending,
   Till earth's constellations are blended in one!

Woman's Love.

There is a balm for hearts grown weary,
   For burning brows that throb with pain,
That cheers though all the world be dreary,
   And gives to life sweet hope again;
How brave the breast this boon possessing,
   Fair gift from angel realms above!
How sad the soul that craves the blessing,
   Or had, but lost a woman's love!

What scene hath charms, though stars are beam-
     ing,
   Though music sweet drifts on the air,
Though ev'ry rose with dew is gleaming,
   Unless the form we love be there?
Let fortune claim my rarest treasure,
   And fame far from my name remove,
I'll say farewell to ev'ry pleasure,
   But spare, oh, spare me woman's love.

The Nameless Valley.

Long years ago, when you and I
    Beside the river wandered free,
You told me that though hope should die
    Yet still your heart would faithful be.
O love, those days have passed away,
    Fond hope hath faded long ago;
Here, all alone, I stand to-day
    And watch the silent river flow.

The green hills keep their vigil still
    Upon the sleeping town below,
And soft the moonlight glints the rill
    As in the nights of long ago;
O love, the fault lies not with you,
    Nor is my weary heart to blame;
But, lo, the watching hills are true,
    The faithful river flows the same!

The Harvest Home.

The harvest has come and the vines hang low,
The fruit on the branches sways to and fro;
The grain is all garnered, we've stacked the hay,
And happy and light are our hearts to-day.

(227)

The harvest has come with its ample yield,
And rich is each meadow and waving field;
The earth is Thy garden, Lord, Thine alone,
'Tis Thou who has blest what our hands have
    sown.

Lord, deep in our hearts sow the seeds of love,
Where sin may not wither, nor sorrow move,
That when Thy bright angels as reapers come,
We'll sing the glad song of our harvest home.

Over the River.

Though seeming dark the waters
    That broad and silent flow,
Though dim the distant haven
    That only faith can show;
Yet fear not, weary pilgrim,
    With Jesus at thy side,
For angel hands will guide thee
    Across the mystic tide.

If those we leave behind us
    The truth could only know,
Then tears of joy, not sorrow,
    Would soothe us when we go;
The farewell kiss at parting
    Would be a brief adieu,
For just across the river
    Our hands will clasp anew.

Easter Carol.

Jesus lives! the vict'ry's won,
  Glory be to God on high!
Sing the praise of Christ, our Lord,
  While angel hosts reply.
Sin and death by Him are conquered,
  All our fears are o'er;
He who died for our redemption
  Lives forever more!
Alleluia! Alleluia! Praise be to God!

Victory! the night is past,
  Brightly gleams the happy day;
March in triumph, doubt no more,
  For Jesus leads the way!
Sing the song of exultation,
  Man from death is free!
Christ, at God's right hand in triumph,
  Reigns eternally!
Alleluia! Alleluia! Praise be to God!

Not Here.

Not here, if you please,
  Where ev'ry one sees
Our acts with an eye microscopic;
  Where ears are agog,
  Like a tar's in a fog,
To catch up a contraband topic.
You will pardon my seeming distrust
  When the point of my hint becomes clear;
Have your say to the end, if you must,
  But beware that you say it not here!

When only a lad,
  And caught by my dad
In mischief, or wickedly larking;
  When laid on his knee
  From the whack I got free
By simply that sentence remarking.
"Oh, not here!" I would cry in alarm,
  While I wriggled and twisted with fear,
Then in pity descended his arm
  At the timely suggestion, not here!

When, later in life,
  I courted my wife,
When dollars and quarters were stinted,
  Those words I would say
  And look the wrong way
If ice cream or candy she hinted.

But a scholar so apt was that miss—
    As the sequel will make it appear—
That whenever I begged for a kiss,
    She would giggle and answer, not here!

Christmas.

O happy, happy festal day,
    O long awaited dawn,
With joy and love we welcome thee,
    O blessed Christmas morn.

Let all the world its homage pay,
    Let loyal voices sing,
For on this day, in Bethlehem,
    Was born a Mighty King.

O joyous morn of peace and love,
    Sweet day of promise bright,
Shed forth in every shadowed life
    Thy warmth and wondrous light.

Let ev'ry heart be thrilled with joy,
    Let care be cast away,
For Christ is here to cheer and bless,
    And this is Christmas day!

Finger-Prints Upon the Pane.

I had opened wide the shutters
  Of the long deserted room,
And a flood of golden sunshine
  Chased away the dreary gloom;
'Twas while gazing round with tenderness
  Where baby last had lain,
That I chanced to see the finger-prints
  Upon the window pane.

Still the empty crib was standing
  In its old accustomed place,
But from 'neath the little blankets
  Peeped no precious infant face.
How I longed to clasp its angel form,
  One more sweet kiss obtain
From the rosy lips that oft had pressed
  Against the window pane.

Oh! my heart seemed almost breaking
  As I gathered from the floor,
Here a shoe and there a stocking
  That my little darling wore;
And I could not, though I loved the room,
  One moment more remain,
Where those snowy hands had left their prints
  Upon the window pane.

Twilight on the Sea.

Now twilight falls upon the sea,
   The wild birds homeward wing their way,
The dew-drops gather on the lea,
   And shadows gloom the fading day.
"Ahoy! Ahoy!" comes faint the cry,
   As nearer speeds the fisher's merry crew;
"Ahoy! Ahoy!" the fond reply,
   From waiting, watching hearts so true.
         And the breakers crash,
            And the breakers roar,
         And the darkness veils
            The landscape o'er.

Oh, happy twilight, calm and sweet,
   That bids the weary world take rest,
The hour that parted loved ones meet
   And peaceful home is doubly blest!
But hark! "Ahoy!" how shrill the cry,
   Now o'er the foaming billows borne!
Good night to joy, to peace good bye;
   O wretched, waiting hearts forlorn.
         And the breakers crash,
            And the breakers roar,
         And the fated crew
            Returns no more.

The Broken Tryst.

Far o'er the hills two pale stars beam,
  Shepherds their flocks are calling;
Out from the cots the lamp lights gleam,
  And night shades fast are falling.
    Lonely wait I trembling here,
    Beats my timid heart with fear;
Wilt thou come, O love, my own?
    I will chide thee not, nor blame;
Come, ere hope with day hath flown,
  Thou wilt find me still the same.

Now must I sadly turn away;
  Oh, that I had one token!
Dim grows the fleeting twilight gray,
  And love's sweet tryst is broken.
    Should we never meet again,
    Dreary would my life be then.
Through long years that come and go,
  Though my days shall lonely be,
Sweetest bliss 'twill be to know
  Once thy thoughts were all for me.

Only Dreaming.

The wild birds are singing,
The merry bells are ringing,
  All the world seems full of glee!
But my poor heart is aching,
And my poor heart is breaking,
  For Jamie's proved false to me.
E'en now to the wedding,
While bitter tears I'm shedding,
  They enter the old church door
Where, oft in my dreaming,
With bright visions beaming,
  I have been the bride before.

The bright sun is beaming,
And merrily is streaming
  Golden rays upon the floor;
Hark! I hear a voice speaking,
The stair with footsteps creaking;
  Surely, someone is at my door!
Oh, why am I sighing?
'Tis Jamie's voice replying
  That he's called me o'er and o'er.
My trouble's but seeming,
The fact is I've been dreaming,
  As I've often dreamt before!

(235)

The New Year.

If we could but count the roses
   That have blossomed through the year,
Or remember all the mornings
   When the sky was bright and clear;
We would bid the old year farewell
   With regretful tears and sighs,
And but deem its many shadows
   Only blessings in disguise.

In the year that lies before us,
   Like a vast and unknown sea,
Lurk the reefs and bloom the islands
   That will make our destiny;
Bravely start upon the voyage,
   And, should e'er you need a chart,
Then take up the old year's lessons
   That are written on your heart.

On life's journey take the bright side,
   Ever try the light to find ;
For to those who face the sunshine
   Ev'ry shadow falls behind.
Trust the good and Mighty Ruler;
   Work and keep a conscience clear,
Then you'll bless the old year's mem'ry,
   Greet with joy the new-born year.

Stay Home To-night With the Old Folks.

Stay home to-night with the old folks,
  Give them an evening's cheer,
For worn are their hearts and weary,
  Toiling for many a year;
Sing them a song that is sweet and low,
One that they sang long, long ago!
Though dim are eyes with watching,
  Though seamed are their brows, once fair,
Though sad be their thoughts to-morrow,
  To-night let them know no care.

Stay home to-night with the old folks,
  Let them be gay once more;
Bring back rosy scenes that have perished,
  Days that forever are o'er;
Sing them a song that is sweet and low,
One that they sang long, long ago!
For love of the hands ever willing,
  The smiles that our childhood knew,
For sake of the lips that have blessed us,
  To-night cheer their hearts so true.

After the Wedding.

The bright stars were timidly peeping
Thro' the rifts in the clouds that were sweeping
O'er the world that lay quietly sleeping,
　　When home from the wedding I came;
The wind thro' the tree-tops was sighing,
And the screech-owl was dismally crying,
While each bush I kept cautiously eying,
　　And edging away from the same.

That night the earth had a queer feeling,
I am sure that the fences were reeling,
And I caught myself frequently kneeling—
　　Inspecting the state of the ground;
Fatigued, I determined on resting—
First the warmth of a pocket-friend testing—
Then myself of my new boots divesting,
　　Dropped into a slumber most sound!

Soon out from the hedge there came crawling,
A most terrible form that kept bawling:
"Oh, somebody'll get a good mauling,
　　For stealing the bed of a ghost!"
'Most dead at its feet I fell pleading,
But the monster my prayer was unheeding,
When I grabbed it—and 'woke with nose bleed-
　　　ing,
　　And found I was hugging a post!

(238)

The Road by the River.

The road by the river is lonely,
    The leaves from the branches are gone;
I hear my sad sigh's echo only
    As the cold waters silent glide on:
There's no smile, no voice to greet me,
    For my loved one's far away,
Yet the joys we've known entreat me,
    And their mem'ries bid me stay.

Then farewell, O river, I leave you,
    Though still drift my thoughts with your tide,
And sweet is the message I give you
    For one who is far from my side;
Tell, oh, tell my love I'm lonely,
    That I'm waiting, watching here,
That the world has one face only
    To my soul forever dear.

The Ribbon She Wore.

I have left a girl behind me
  Who is sweeter than a rose,
And her gentle heart I know is warm and true;
  And wherever fate may find me
  In my breast shall still repose,
This dear little piece of faded ribbon blue.

      Love from her eyes is beaming,
        She is pure and fair;
      And I'll keep this bit of ribbon
      Till we meet, because I know
        She wore it in her hair.

When the stars above are beaming
  In the silent summer sky,
Then in fancy I again am at her side;
  Still of her I'm fondly dreaming
  As the days glide slowly by,
For she promised that she'd be my loving bride.

I have left a girl behind me,
  · And she's singing all the day
Like the merry birds that cleave the sunny air;
  And one thing shall e'er remind me
  Of our love, and cheer my way,
'Tis the ribbon that she twined among her hair.

Pretty Wild Roses.

Pretty wild roses bring me,
   Gathered by the way;
In them love reposes,
And their blush discloses
What your heart proposes,
Pretty, shell-pink roses
Bring them fresh with morning dew,
   Gathered by the way.
Timidly, down by the hedges,
   Watching the trav'lers pass by,
List'ning to true lovers' pledges,
   Hearing the wayfarer's sigh—
Beautiful, fragrant roses,
   Blooming wild and free,
Emblem of fond devotion,
   Gather them, love, for me:
Pretty wild roses bring me,
   Pluck them by the way;
Let their sweet breath tell me
   What your lips would say.

Pretty wild roses fading
   By the dusty way;
Sad the winds are sighing,
Birds are southward flying,

No loved voice replying
Is to cheer me trying,
And the roses withered lie
  By the dusty way.
Lonely they droop by the hedges,
  Weary the trav'lers pass by;
No more are heard love's fond pledges,
  Clouds gather dark in the sky—
Yet will I love my roses
  Though they seared may be;
Still will their petals yellow
  Treasures prove to me:
Pretty wild roses ever,
  Though you fade away,
For your leaves still tell me
  What my love would say.

The Turning in the Lane.

Oh, brother, if you're weary,
   If your feet are bruised and sore,
Just think how oft have pilgrims
   Trod the same hard road before;
And if your heart should falter,
   Still be brave, and try again,
For perhaps you may to-morrow
   Reach the turning in the lane.

Your sky may be o'erclouded,
   Chill and dark the gloomy day;
Yet, brother, still remember,
   Ev'ry storm must pass away:
The friends of sunny summer
   Their old warmth may not retain,
But all will gladly greet you
   At the turning of the lane.

Only a Tramp.

" 'Tis only a tramp," I heard them say,
As the cold, still form in the moonlight lay;
The shoeless feet all bruised and torn,
The garments soiled and travel worn,
The youthful face with its lines of care
And the dark brown mass of matted hair,
All told the tale in a quiet way,
Of a homeless lad and a life astray.

Once, in a mansion, far away,
In the arms of a mother an infant lay;
And oft did the woman in holy bliss
The rosy lips of her darling kiss:
Then the child grew up in his strength and pride,
Then wandered off from the matron's side—
But, seen in the glare of the watchman's lamp,
E'en his mother would say, " 'tis only a tramp."

The Toll-Taker.

(From the Operetta, " A Jolly Christmas Eve.")

In a neat little cot by the wayside,
　　Daddy Wicket, the toll-taker, lives,
And each trav'ler who rides o'er the turnpike,
　　A mite to the toll-taker gives;
He holds out his hand very graceful,
　　While a twinkle is seen in his eye,
And he says a kind word to all comers,
　　And he smiles as they swiftly glide by.

When the sun o'er the hill-top is peeping,
　　When all sweet is the flower-kissed air,
When the day goes to rest in the gloaming,
　　Still dear Daddy Wicket is there;
He stands in the door of the toll-house,
　　Or he sits on his three-legged chair,
And his pride is to care for a stranger,
　　Yet is he quite a stranger to care.

Oh, then, who can forget Daddy Wicket,
　　Or the wonderful shake of his head ?
He who oft gives the homeless a shelter,
　　Who oft hungry mortals has fed!
Oh, may we, as through life we journey,
　　Never meet with a less noble soul
Than the friend and the joy of our childhood,
　　Daddy Wicket, who gathers the toll.

(245)

Daddy Wicket.

(From the Operetta, " A Jolly Christmas Eve.")

My name's Henry Philip Magonigal Wicket,
  And you'll say that it's not very short;
So my name being long, why, the children, to
    nick it,
  Call me old Daddy Wicket in sport.
I gather great hatfuls of pennies and nickels
  From people that drive on the pike;
I sigh when luck frowns, and I laugh when it
    tickles,
  And I do pretty much as I like.

My name's Henry Philip Magonigal Wicket,
  'Twould be foolish the same to deny;
And I " save at the bung," but I " waste at the
    spigot,"
  Which is why such a poor man am I.
I'd rather be poor than to be rich and stingy,
  I'd rather be good than be bad,
And that's why I live in a hut small and dingy,
  Because I make sad people glad.

The Grocer's Song.

(From the Operetta, " Holly Berries.")

HE.

I'm a grocer and keep at the corner,
    I'm a judge of a ham or a cheese,
I can wait on a dozen together,
    And can answer them all with great ease.
When the little boy comes with his story,
    For his bread and his ounce of green tea,
When he says he's forgotten the money,
    Why, his motive I plainly can see.

SHE.

He's a grocer for all there is in it,
    He is posted on bushels and pecks,
He can sell you potatoes and apples,
    And hide from your view their black specks;
His mackerel never are rusty,
    For he scrapes all the brown rust away;
Oh, the bus'ness has many a secret,
    But I think I'll not tell them to-day.

HE.

The McFaddens all thought they were poisoned,
    When for onions I sent them, instead,
A string of rank garlic, which tasting,
    McFadden declared he was dead.

(247)

I will own that I've measured molasses
  By mistake in an oily tin can,
But "to err," says the poet, "is human,"
  And a grocer is only a man.

BOTH.

Yes, we know ev'ry trick of the bus'ness,
  Moldy codfish we make good as new;

SHE.

But we never put sand in the sugar,

BOTH.

And I'll prove it, my darling, by you!

HE.

We take pride in good weight and full measure,
  And our scales and our measures are true—

BOTH.

And I'll prove it, I'll prove it, my darling,
  Yes, I'll prove it, my darling, by you!

He's a Man Among a Hundred.

(From the Operetta, "Holly Berries.")

He's a man among a hundred,
  He is careful, he is keen,
He can sing a song or whistle,
  He's as good as I have seen;
No one could be more obliging,
  And, what's better still than all,
He found those holly berries
  That are hanging on the wall.

He's a man among a hundred,
  Warm of heart, with head quite cool;
One can see by what he's shown us
  That he's neither knave nor fool;
One and all, I'm sure, we like him,
  Him our friend we'll always call,
For he found those holly berries
  That are hanging on the wall.

Maybe there's a stray dog-berry,
  Maybe some cranberries, too,
E'en a lot of wee tea-berries,
  Bits of laurel not a few;
Yet we take his good intentions,
  Though the lot he brought is small,
For he found what holly berries
  There are hanging on the wall.

(249)

A Father's Love.

(From the Opera, " Flogeo.")

A father's love though most revealed
　In moments bright and fair,
Yet warmer glows when 'tis concealed
　Beneath a cloud of care;
The weight of toil alone he bears,
　That ours may lighter be,
And oft his heart a fetter wears,
　That ours may beat more free;
Then let us greet him with a smile,
　Make smooth his path to-day;
For 'tis but yet a little while
　When he must pass away.

A father's love though seldom sung,
　Is pure and dear to me;
The name lisped by my childish tongue,
　Still loved and prized shall be.
A mother's love like ivy clings
　And binds us all in one;
But his, the oak that shelter flings,
　His glance, our summer sun.
Then let us greet him with a smile,
　Make smooth his path to-day;
For 'tis but yet a little while
　When he must pass away.

(250)

Serenade.

(From the Opera, " Flogeo.")

Lady, if thou art awake,
    To thy lover make reply;
Come, Oh, come, for love's sweet sake,
    Nor my pleading heart deny.
Lady fair, if thou dost sleep,
    Then may angels pure and bright
Tender vigil o'er thee keep
    Through the silent hours of night.

Lady mine, to thee I sing;
    Canst thou not one sweet word say?
Will my voice no answer bring,
    Must I sadly turn away?
Come, Oh, come, my loved one true,
    Let me ask thee not in vain,
Or if dreaming then adieu,
    Till I see thy face again.

The Old Philosopher.

(From the Opera, " Flogeo.")

E'en the best of roads are rocky and rough
  To the feet that tramp alone,
And the richest man is needy enough
  Who can call no heart his own;
Of the hundred hands that warmly we shake
  We are lucky if one there be
That would grasp as tight for charity's sake,
  Did they know our poverty.

'Tis a world of show, of hollow deceit,
  'Tis a world both pure and bright;
'Tis a paradox, a riddle complete
  That but few can read aright;
E'en the longest life must knuckle at last,
  And recline on its couch of clay;
And a fool is he who has gold amassed
  For the wise to scatter gay.

A Widow of Forty-two.

(From the Opera, " Flogeo.")

I'm only a widow of forty-two,
But that is a secret for me, not you;
There's many a maiden of twenty-three
Who'd look like an owl if compared with me:
If not young and blushing, I'm stout and fair,
With not yet the sign of a silver hair—
'Tis few that would marry if men but knew
Just when a sweet widow is forty-two.

'Tis true I'm a widow of forty-two,
Yet still I've the power to coo and woo;
I've proof that I know how the thing is done,
For haven't I captured my number one?
I'm careful indeed to preserve my looks,
And faces of men I can read like books;
Then why should I bother or make ado
When I'm but a widow of forty-two?

Memorial Day.

Like stars that sink into the west,
  So one by one we seek our rest;
The column's brave and steady tread,
  With banners streaming overhead,
Will still keep step, as in the past,
  Until the rear-guard comes at last.

Ah, yes, like stars we take our flight,
  And whisper, one by one, "Good-night;"
Yet in the light of God's bright day,
  Triumphant, each again will say,
" Hail, Comrade, here has life begun,
  The battle's fought, the victory's won ! "

Jesus, Guard Us Through the Night.

Jesus, guard us through the night,
  Grant us peace, subdue our fears;
Watch us till the silv'ry light
  Of the coming day appears.
Watch us though the sky be dark,
  Though Thy face we cannot see;
To our cry, O Saviour, hark,
  Near to rescue ever be.

Jesus, guard us while we sleep,
  While the world in slumber lies;
In Thy fold we fain would keep,
  Watched by legions from the skies.
Though our heads may lowly rest,
  Though on splendor's couch repose;
Let our sleep with peace be blest,
  Save us, Jesus, from our foes.

The Minstrel.

If you sing the songs I've sung you,
  If you whisper but the air,
Then, believe me, in the spirit
  With my song, I'm with you there.

I am with you—ever with you;
  At your side by night, by day;
In the crowded street at noontime,
  In the dark and lonesome way.

For the songs I love to sing you
  Of my soul are but a part,
And they float like burning incense
  From the censer of my heart.

www.ingramcontent.com/pod-product-compliance
Lightning Source LLC
Chambersburg PA
CBHW031427020726
47499CB00005B/1628